CLAIMED BY THE FIRE DRAGON PRINCE

ARIA WINTER

JADE WALTZ

Purple Fall
Publishing

Published in the United States by Purple Fall Publishing. Purple Fall Publishing and the Purple Fall Publishing Logos are trademarks and/or registered trademarks of Purple Fall Publishing LLC.- purplefallpublishing.com

Publisher's Cataloging-in-Publication data

Names: Winter, Aria, author. | Waltz, Jade, author.

Title: Claimed by the Fire Dragon Prince / Aria Winter & Jade Waltz.

Series: Elemental Dragon Warriors

Description: Purple Fall Publishing, 2020.

Identifiers: ISBN:

978-1-64253-237-1 (pbk.)

978-1-64253-404-7 (ebook)

978-1-64253-264-7 (audio)

Subjects: LCSH Space exploration--Fiction. | Human-alien encounters--Fiction. | Dragons--Fiction. | Shapeshifting--Fiction. | Science fiction. | Romance fiction. | BISAC FICTION / Science Fiction / Alien Contact | FICTION / Romance / Science Fiction | FICTION / Romance / Paranormal / Shifters

Classification: LCC PS3623 .I6675 C53 2020 | DDC 813.6--dc23

Cover Design by Kim Cunningham of Atlantis Book Design

PRINTED IN THE UNITED STATES OF AMERICA

Dedication

To my husband: Thank you for all your love and support. You are not just my husband, you are my best friend and my rock. I love you more than anything.
-AW

To My Husband,
Thank you for being my support and rock during this writing journey.
I love you!
-Jade

CONTENTS

CHAPTER 1

LILLIANA

Alarms blare throughout the ship, muting the distant screams that echo down the hallways. Dark smoke fills the corridors, stinging my eyes and burning my lungs with each inhalation. I lift my arm and fist the fabric of my sleeve to cover my mouth and nose. I'm not sure if it actually filters the air I breathe, but it makes me feel a little better about running in the opposite direction of the escape pods.

We've practiced orderly evacuation of an unsalvageable ship dozens of times in anticipation of this exact scenario. Despite all our training, it's absolute chaos as people rush past me, frantic to reach the escape pods. A deafening boom splits the air as the pirates fire another blast at the hull, rocking the ship violently. I don't know what species our attackers are, but they are hideous to behold. Ugly, humanoid lizard aliens with yellow, vertically slit pupils that stared menacingly at the viewscreen as they demanded our surrender only moments ago.

I make my way toward the bridge. The doors are ajar, a low buzzing hum emanating from the control panel as they struggle to close. I push through the narrow opening then gasp as my eyes scan the room. The scent of smoke and iron fills the air so thick, I can taste it on my tongue. A wave of nausea rolls through me and I swallow against the bile rising in my throat.

Half the crew is slumped over their stations, dead—including our Captain.

Tears sting my eyes, but I blink them back. I only just spoke to her this morning about converting one of the cargo bays to a dedicated vegetable garden. She clapped a hand on my shoulder, praising the plan that would have increased our food production capabilities by at least fifteen percent.

My gaze sweeps to the navigation console and relief washes through me. Skye isn't there at her station.

Hope soars. My best friend must be alive and evacuating to the escape pods.

Another explosion sounds along the hull, vibrating the entire ship. I lose my balance and pitch forward. Gripping the chair in front of me, I barely manage to remain upright. I have to get out of here. I'm a botanist, not an engineer, so I don't know how much more damage our vessel can take before she breaks apart. But if I had to guess, I would say catastrophic failure is imminent, as is the death of all remaining crew.

I rush toward the door and back into the hallway. I'm not ready to die today. My pulse pounds in my ears as I race down the corridor. My feet cannot carry me fast enough from the sound of blaster fire and the shouts that ring out behind me.

The pirates must have boarded. Judging by the damage they've already caused, their technology is superior and we're heavily outgunned. So, the fact that they bothered to board means they don't just want our cargo and our ship; they want us. Otherwise, why not just destroy the ship? Fire enough holes to vent us all into space so they can claim their loot?

The sight of a familiar figure up ahead lends me a burst of speed. It's my best friend, Skye, sitting in the middle of the corridor and leaning over someone. Her normally long golden hair is streaked red with blood.

"Skye!"

She lifts her tear-filled gaze to mine, and I inhale sharply when I notice her younger brother covered in blood, his head in her lap. He lies with an unnatural stillness that stops my heart. I notice the slight blue-gray tinge of his lips and realize his blue eyes are open but unseeing. She stares down at him in dismay.

"Skye, we have to get to the escape pods."

"I can't leave Thomas," her voice quavers softly as a tear slips down her cheek. "I can't, Lilly."

I grip her forearm. "He's gone, Skye! We have to leave! Now!"

Her gaze meets mine with a faraway look as she nods shakily. Carefully, she removes Thomas' head from her lap then leans over his still form. She reaches out and gently closes his eyes before placing a tender kiss on his forehead. "I love you, Thomas," she whispers. "I'm so sorry."

Tears of pain and anger stream down my cheeks as I stare down at the lifeless form of my best friend's brother. Why him? How can fate be so cruel?

Another loud *boom* reverberates along the hull, snapping me back to alertness. I take Skye's hand in mine and meet her eyes steadily. "We have to go. Now."

She stands and I tug on her arm, dragging her along behind me as we rush down the hallway.

The caustic burn of adrenaline pumps through my veins,

granting me sharp mental clarity amid the chaos that surrounds us when we reach the escape pods. People are injured and bleeding, their expressions frozen in shock. Officers rush back and forth, herding and loading what's left of the crew into the vessels we hoped never to use.

Perhaps it was hubris, but I know I wasn't alone in the belief that nothing could ever touch us. Our ship was designed by the best minds our planet had to offer. No expense was spared in the construction of the strong and formidable colonization fleet. Our mission's cargo was the most precious thing our dying planet had left.

We are the last of our kind. Earth has been destroyed and our civilization is gone.

"Lilly!"

My head snaps toward the sound of my name and relief fills me when I find Anna.

"Over here! Quick!"

Pulling Skye's arm, I guide her toward the escape pod. Still in shock, she offers little resistance as I drag her behind me. I place her in the seat next to Anna, strapping her harness tightly across her chest.

Anna's green eyes snap up to meet mine. "Where's Thomas?" she asks, knowing Skye would never leave her younger brother behind. He was the only family she had left.

Emotions lodge in my throat but I somehow manage to speak around them. "He's not coming."

Her gaze sweeps back to the door as if expecting him to show up. "What are you talking about? What do you mean 'he's not coming'?"

I shake my head slightly, biting my lower lip to stop it from quivering.

Anna is a doctor. Death is nothing new to her. With a slight clench of her jaw, she blinks back tears. "What about Talia and Milo? Did you see them anywhere?"

I curse under my breath. I didn't think to even look for them. My sole focus was on finding Skye and Thomas. We've looked out for each other since we all lost our parents three years ago.

The four of us—Skye, Anna, Talia, and I—have been best friends since childhood, shortly after we set out on the mission.

Of all of us, Talia is the only one whose family is still intact. I expected to find her here with her parents and brother, Milo. "You haven't seen them?" I ask in alarm.

She shakes her head. "I thought they'd be here," she says. "Her dad is one of the officers, so I just assumed—"

She breaks off abruptly as her gaze sweeps to the door behind me. I spin to find Talia and Milo rushing toward us. Her eyes are wide in fear. "Have you seen my parents?"

"No," I reply quickly. "They must be in one of the other escape pods."

"They wouldn't leave us behind," she snaps, and then turns to her brother. "Milo, we have to go back! We can't leave without them!"

He shakes his head. "We can't, Talia. The corridor to our quarters has already been sealed."

I inhale sharply as the gravity of his statement hits me. Parts of the ship only seal off when there's been a catastrophic hull breach. My dad, who was an engineer, told me it was one of the many safety functions built into the ship's automated systems. If their parents were in a breached sector, they're already dead. Milo's eyes meet mine and it's easy to see that he's reached the same conclusion. Talia, however, refuses to believe it.

"Let me go, Milo! We have to go back!"

He grips her shoulders firmly. "We can't, Talia! It's suicide to go back there!"

"I don't care!" she cries out.

I take her hand and meet her gaze evenly. "Your parents might have made it to one of the pods that already left." The words are like bitter acid on my tongue. I know I'm probably only giving her false hope. Milo's eyes meet mine and an unspoken understanding passes between us. He knows what I'm doing and why. Their parents would never have evacuated without their children. However, I need to convince Talia to stay here. Rushing back into the ship could kill her. "The pirates have already boarded, and we need to leave before they reach us. Alright?"

She nods reluctantly and takes the seat beside Skye. Both watch the door as if half-expecting the people they love to appear at any moment. I swallow against the lump in my throat, put there by the knowledge that they never will.

Reaching up, I tie my long crimson hair in a loose knot at the nape of my neck. My gaze sweeps over the cabin, trying to determine who else has made it.

On this colony ship, everyone knows everyone. We've been traveling together on the same vessel for years. I think of all the crew I found dead on the bridge and wonder how many friends and colleagues I've lost.

From what I could tell in the chaos, at least three other pods had already ejected by the time we arrived. The escape pods are meant to fit sixty people and this one is a little less than half-full.

My green eyes reflect in the clear, polished metal panels as I stare at the floor, pushing my hands into my lap to still their trembling. I shake my head, hoping this is all a vivid nightmare. Deep down, I already know this is horribly real.

I push down my fear and pain as I force myself to focus. We still have crew left on the ship. I stand and start for the door, wanting to help usher people onto the pods. We need to evacuate as many as we can.

"Where are you going?" Anna calls out behind me.

I turn to face her. "I'm going to help load people into the pods."

I know it's dangerous, and so does she. But I can't just stay here and do nothing.

"I'm coming with you," she says, but I shake my head softly.

"You can't. Each pod needs a doctor and you're the only one here. They can't launch without you."

For safety, each pod must have an assortment of what is considered "essential" personnel.

"You're a botanist," she counters, but I point a finger at Paul. As head of my department, he worked under me. He's just as capable as I am of analyzing soil samples and determining which of the emergency seeds to plant and where.

She gives me a reluctant nod. "Be careful!"

"I will," I promise.

I turn back and head for the door. Just as I reach the threshold, the hatch slams shut.

"Wait!" I cry out, frantically banging on the tiny window. "It's only half full!"

The officer doesn't even turn in my direction, but the airlock hasn't been sealed off yet.

I press my palm against the access panel, hoping it will respond. A red light flashes across the screen, indicating an error in processing my command.

I yell at the glass, desperate to get someone's attention. "Don't launch! We still have room!"

On the other side, I notice my coworker, Abby, with a bag slung over her shoulder and her two-year-old daughter, Kayla, on her hip. Her eyes are wide with panic as the airlock doors seal shut between us. "No!"

A high-pitched hum vibrates my eardrums a moment before the pod ejects violently, jerking and spinning away from the ship. Pain explodes across the back of my skull as I slam against the far wall. My limbs feel heavy and numb as I struggle to right myself, to no avail. My head spins and darkness creeps into the edges of my vision. Rough hands grip me firmly, strapping a harness around my body that refuses to move.

"Thank you," I barely manage. My eyes blink open and my gaze drifts to the hatch window as we tumble away into the dark void of space.

Flashing red lights and piercing sirens fill the air as the pod's computer lists a series of damage warnings over the speakers. Through the thick mental fog clouding my brain, I'm unable to register what most of it means. But judging by the panicked expressions of the people around me, I know it's not good.

Barely able to keep my eyes open, I struggle to remain conscious. Another explosion rocks the hull.

"They're firing on the escape pods!" someone yells. "We're not going to make it!"

A moment of clarity sharpens my mind. Why am I fighting to stay awake if we're about to die? I'd rather be asleep for this part. Closing my eyes, the sounds of distant cries follow me as I fall away into oblivion.

CHAPTER 2

VARUS

I was never supposed to rule.

That duty belonged to my older sister, Laris. It's been three cycles since the plague swept through our world, taking her life and the lives of over half our females, leaving most of the few who survived barren.

Closing my eyes, I can still picture my sister. Reflective green eyes so like my own. The deep-crimson scales we both inherited from our mother and the proud, spiraling black horns that swept back from her head, as long as our father's. Many commented that Laris and I could have been twins, we were so similar in appearance. I used to tease her that my tail was longer and the spines down my back and tail were much sharper than hers.

I find myself thinking of her every day since she passed. The pain of her loss has faded over the past few cycles, but the echoes still linger, and I suspect they will forever remain.

Our fate was determined by the Gods long before we were born.

My father's voice surfaces in my mind. It is how he accepts the loss of his beloved daughter.

If that is true, then where are these Gods? Why do we pray to them when they do not answer?

I've often wondered if the plague was punishment for the violence of our ancestors. They waged countless wars against other races, against one another, even.

My race was once unified until we split into the four elemental Clans over a thousand cycles ago. We may differ from each other now, but in the past, we all lived as one people. And over the cycles, we've fought and killed one another in violent, bloody wars.

What a terrible crime we committed against our makers. Extinguishing life that has been granted by the Gods, all in the name of expanding territory and avenging trivial offenses.

Standing on the balcony, I search the stars, looking for guidance I doubt will ever come. I am to be betrothed soon, to the princess of the Water Clan. How strange our pairing will be since she is of Water and my people are born of Fire.

I turn my gaze to the city below my balcony and the many vacant holes lining the cliffside. These dwellings used to be full of life. Instead of bright lights within, flickering behind the tapestries that once proudly labeled their property's entrance, darkness fills the spaces. We lost so many, first to the wars and then to the plague.

Various buildings and houses formed from earthen brown and red clay stand proudly atop the mesa. The style is simple yet elegant in its design and modeled after our castle.

The wealthy make their homes up here, while the majority of our citizens live in the valley below, along the river that curves around the mesa's base. Verdant fields of rich farmlands, fed from the water's canals, dot the landscape. Across the river lies a steep plateau. The deep orange and crimson layers of rock are beautiful even in the darkness.

Visitors from other tribes often remark on how harsh life here must be, but I've never found this to be truth. The great desert beyond the city is an ocean of red sand; so dry, it was once believed to be devoid of life. But in the hundreds of cycles we've made our home here, we've learned the secrets buried in the fine, crimson grains of earth. A system of caves, connected beneath the surface, flows with vast, deep rivers of water. There is a plethora of life to be found here, if one knows where to look.

I often fly over the desert at night, marveling at the various creatures that move and hunt along the dunes. I wonder if my soon-to-be mate will recognize my home's beauty, or if she will miss the great oceans that line the cliffs near her home.

I sigh heavily. We have no choice, she and I. With so few females left, the discord between our Clans must end. To broker peace, we will attempt what I never would have thought possible before the plague claimed so many of our people.

We will forge treaties and alliances with the other Clans through bonding. The first pairing of this design will be mine and Noralla's. I will do my best to be a good mate to the Water Princess. I only hope that this life will make her happy.

Though she is of easy nature and pleasing to look upon, in her eyes I see the lingering doubt she tries so hard to hide. I recognize it because the same doubt has shone back at me in the mirror every day since my father negotiated our betrothal with her Clan.

I am Fire and she is Water. Were two elementals ever so completely opposite from each other?

Shaking my head, I look at my hands. I suppose we will find out soon enough.

A flash of light in the distance draws my attention. I look to the sky and my mouth drops open when a trail of fire blazes across the desert plains. It is not uncommon for meteorite debris to penetrate the atmosphere, but this one is larger than any I've seen.

A strange warmth blooms in my chest as I watch it fall.

I've heard stories of those who could sense their destiny calling to them, but I have never put much faith in these tales, believing them to be the musings of spiritualists and dreamers. And yet, I cannot ignore this strange compulsion as the space between my two hearts grows warm, where my scales would glow brightly if I found my fated one.

I've always been curious, an explorer. The unknown fascinates me. Even without the odd reaction my body has to this blazing meteorite, something about it calls to me and I must know why. I cannot push aside the gnawing feeling that this falling star is important. I trust my intuition. It has directed my path to my favor many times before, so I will not ignore it now.

My thoughts turn briefly to the betrothal ceremony and a heavy sigh escapes me. I know I have a duty to my family and our kingdom. But I must know what fell from the sky this night; I will not be at peace until I have an answer.

With a slight clench of my jaw, I cast my gaze out to the desert again and resolve to leave in the morning to investigate.

CHAPTER 3

LILLIANA

"Lilliana?" a familiar voice sounds in my ear. "Wake up. Are you all right?"

A low groan escapes me as I open my eyes. Stabs of pain pierce my forehead when blinding light assaults my vision. I squint up at Skye as she grabs my hand to pull me into a seated position.

I wince at the movement. Everything hurts, my head most of all.

She gives me a pained smile, drawing my attention to the dark bruise on her chin. "Thank the Stars you're awake. I was so worried." Her voice is thick with emotion as she pulls me into a hug. "Anna told me you'd be all right, but I was terrified of losing you, too."

I swallow the knot of grief in my throat as the image of her brother, Thomas, floats to the surface of my mind. "What happened? Where are we?"

"We crashed. And... I don't know where we are." She shakes her head, resigned. "I don't think anyone does."

Anxiety fills me as I quickly scan the area, only now noticing at least five people lying on the ground and the rest bruised, limping, or injured like my best friend. However, I can't spot Talia, Milo, or Anna. "Where are—"

Already anticipating my question, Skye cuts me off. "Everyone survived." Her eyes dart to the side. "Some are still unconscious, but Anna has scanned everyone, and we should all be fine."

A heavy sigh of relief escapes me, cut off halfway by a hiss at the sharp pain in my ribs. I band an arm across my torso as if that will somehow ease the deep ache. Since I couldn't care less about modesty at this point, I lift my shirt and notice several dark bruises covering my body. No wonder everything hurts.

Talia appears at the edge of my vision. "Hey!" she calls out, looking no worse for wear as she stands beside her brother, who appears equally unaffected. "I'm so glad you're finally awake."

I blink up at her. "How long have we been here?"

"About twelve hours, give or take," Milo replies. He glances over his shoulder. "Some of us are already putting together some makeshift structures for shelter."

Despite their unscathed appearances, it is easy to see the sadness in their normally sparkling blue eyes. I can only imagine what they're going through, not knowing for sure what happened to their parents.

Anna drops to her knees on my other side. "Hey." She gives me a warm smile in greeting as she runs a scanner over my body. "I'm glad you're up. How do you feel?"

I press my palm to my forehead and wince at the slight pain in my wrist. How am I supposed to feel—great? "Like I crashed on a strange planet," I give her a half-teasing, half-annoyed reply.

A soft laugh escapes her. "You're lucky. I see you still have your sense of humor and nothing is broken. So, you should be fine. It doesn't look like the pirates followed us here, thank goodness."

That's a relief. "What about the other escape pods?"

She shakes her head softly. "No sign of anyone but the twenty-five of us. Though they could have landed further from here. I mean, who knows how big this planet is."

"The pod's computer?" I ask. That's the only way we can locate the other escape vessels if they didn't land nearby.

Anna sighs heavily. "It's fried beyond repair, according to our resident computer specialist." She looks to Skye.

Skye was part of the ship's bridge crew. She may have specialized in navigation, but she knew the computers like the back of her hand. If she says the pod's computer is unsalvageable, I have no reason to doubt her.

"Yeah," Skye adds. "We're lucky we made it." Grief flits briefly across her expression as she corrects herself. "Most of us, anyway."

I reach out and take her hand in mine, giving it a reassuring squeeze. We've both lost people we love. We'll get through this, though it will be hard at first. That's the nature of grieving.

"Everyone has been waiting for you to wake up," Anna says, pulling me back from my melancholy thoughts.

"Me? Why me?"

Skye's gaze travels over our people for a moment before she leans in. "Since you were the director of the botany lab, that makes you the most senior crew member on our escape pod. So…"

"So, what?" I ask incredulously. "That makes me our leader?" I look around. I'm only twenty-three. I'm not the oldest refugee here by far, but it seems everyone decided to choose me by rank.

I've always enjoyed the quiet aspect of my profession. Not

much drama, not much talking. Just me and the plants, one on one. Though I had staff under me, my subordinates felt the same way. Working with plants, watching them grow, and developing new ways to increase crop yield are all inherently relaxing tasks, so managing botanists was never difficult for me. But becoming a leader? I'm not so sure.

That's when it hits me. My jaw drops as I scan the landscape beyond the small circle of my friends. "Did we crash in a desert?"

Skye sighs. "It sure looks that way."

"Red sand and rock as far as the eye can see," Milo tells me with a half-hearted smile.

"Why couldn't we have landed on some sort of tropical island?" Talia laments.

"Or in a beautiful green forest," Anna adds.

Skye lifts a thoughtful gaze to the sky. "For some reason, I always thought we'd end up in a place with lots of water and vegetation."

Well, any other situation would seem ideal compared to ours. But, at least, we all survived and landed on a planet with a breathable atmosphere and tolerable gravity.

I look up at my friends. "Has anyone taken an inventory of our supplies? Food? Water?"

Anna nods. "It looks like we have enough food and water for a month, but after that, we're going to need a new source."

I allow my gaze to drift over the red desert plains that surround us. Rock formations like skeletal islands amid an ocean of sand tower in the distance. A dry wind blows through my hair, carrying a soft scent of something akin to spice and cinnamon. If not for the smell, I could imagine we were back on Earth.

I can see why the others immediately began working on constructing temporary shelters. Our escape pod is mostly intact but the gray tarp flapping over a gaping hole in the side tells me it will never suffice as a permanent shelter. I turn to Anna. "What about the seed banks?"

"One of the first things I thought of, too," she grins. "They survived the crash just fine."

Thank goodness. This means we have a chance to survive. Those seeds are genetically engineered to grow and prosper in even the most extreme environmental conditions. As my eyes sweep over the sand once more, I'm thinking this definitely counts as a harsh and extreme environment.

I notice John, one of the ship's engineers, standing apart from the group. I climb to my feet, intending to speak to him, but my legs wobble and I nearly fall before Milo grips my arms tightly, helping me regain my balance.

"Be careful," he grins. "You just woke up, remember?"

As if I could forget. Part of me still hopes I'm asleep in my bed on the ship and all of this is simply a nightmare.

Just in case, I pinch my forearm, but no luck. This isn't a dream; it's our new reality.

"John!" I call out and he rushes over, probably because he sees Skye standing beside me. He's always had feelings for her, I think—unrequited ones. Skye went on one date with him, which was enough to tell her what kind of person he was. The first question he asked was how long her brother would be sharing her quarters. After their parents died, Thomas was all the family she had left, and she resented his comment suggesting that he was nothing but a burden.

Tim joins him, his eyes raking over my body like I'm the best thing he's ever seen. He worked security on the ship. Sure, he's handsome and his body is toned, but he also carries a reputation as a womanizer.

I suspect the only reason he's so interested in me is that I'm the only woman who has refused an invitation to dinner with him. He's so handsome I almost agreed, but then he commented that he'd happily make us breakfast in the morning as well. That ruined him for me. It may be a ridiculous, romantic fantasy, but I've always wanted my first time to be special. I wasn't interested in becoming another notch in his belt, so I turned him down.

"You're up!" Tim flashes his signature boyish grin. "I was worried about you."

Despite my best efforts to appear completely uninterested, my cheeks heat under the intense scrutiny of his deep, blue eyes. I'm still human and he *is* handsome; he's just not for me. I want romance, not lust. "Have you seen any signs of indigenous life? Anything around the perimeter of our"—my eyes sweep over our wrecked escape pod and the small patch of survivors—"camp that might be a threat?"

His upbeat expression falters. He gives me a nervous grin as he rubs the back of his neck. "I, uh, hadn't really gotten around to checking on anything yet."

"Alright, I need you to get on that. We don't want to be surprised by a predator or something."

He nods and I look to John. "What about the rovers? Did they survive the crash?"

"Yeah. Both did."

I lift my gaze to the blazing, orange sun overhead, burning brightly in the pale-blue sky, then back down at him. "Did you lay out the day panels to charge the rovers and the rest of the emergency equipment?"

He shakes his head.

"Let's get started on that," I tell him. He nods and leaves.

In the back of my mind, I'm surprised by how easily issuing orders comes to me. Then again, I'm also taken aback that I'm the first one to ask these questions. How could an engineer and a security officer not think of implementing such basic measures? I've always marveled at how some people have to be prodded into action.

On the other hand, Milo and a few others started working on temporary shelters, without being told to because they realized shelter was a priority for our survival.

I turn to Anna. "How are we doing on medical supplies?"

"The kit survived the crash intact," she answers, shooting me a hesitant look as I turn toward the wrecked escape pod. "You should probably rest a bit longer. You just woke up, you know."

I throw another cursory glance at the people around me. Some still lie unconscious on the ground while a few others suffer from wounds that are heavily bandaged. I'm lucky I survived relatively unscathed, with a few aches and bruises but no serious injury.

"No," I tell Anna. "I want to see exactly what we're working with here. Then we need to figure out how to establish a permanent settlement."

"Permanent?" Talia asks.

"These escape pods were only meant for a one-way trip. Even *if* it was intact, it couldn't break the atmosphere to get us back into space." I allow my gaze to drift over the dunes that surround us. "For better or worse, this is it—we're home now. So, we need to find a way to survive here. I don't know about you, but I'm thinking our best bet is not out in the open." I pause. "If this planet is anything like Earth, there could be sandstorms here, and I'd rather not be caught in one if we can help it."

She nods, but I read the disappointment in her eyes. "What if one of the colony ships survived the attack?" She lifts her gaze to the sky. "What if they're still up there somewhere?"

My heart stops. "The transmitter beacon. Is it on?"

She frowns. "Of course. That's one of the first things John switched on after we crashed. Why?"

"Shut it off! Now!"

My friends look stunned, but Milo rushes to the wreckage to do what I've asked.

"Why are you—" Anna starts, but I cut her off with my answer.

"If one of our ships survived the attack, the pirates could have, too. And if they went to all this trouble to attack us, they might still be looking for us." Suddenly, finding a permanent settlement with better cover seems exponentially more important.

"But what about the other escape pods? Without the computer, the beacon is their only way to find us."

I shake my head. "Hopefully, they've shut their beacons off, too. We can't risk alerting the pirates of our location. We can consider switching the transmitter on in a few days, but not yet." I turn to address all my friends. "Once the rovers are charged, we should set out to investigate those rock formations," I point into the distance. "See if there are any caves we can use for shelter. Who knows, we might even find a source of water. I'll run some tests on the soil as well. If we can start planting something now, the crops will be ready long before we run out of rations."

If we happen to run into a sentient species, I can only hope they're friendly instead of hostile like the pirates. However, I don't voice that thought aloud because I don't want to incite panic. We already have enough problems without speculating on worst-case scenarios.

As I study the light-blue sky, I almost expect to see a ship breaking through the atmosphere, but only a thin wisp of gray clouds hangs overhead. I pray we shut the signal off in time. We have no hope of defending ourselves against an assault from an obviously superior species.

CHAPTER 4

VARUS

I t is the day of my betrothal ceremony, but I will not participate. If it is my fate to be mated to a female to forge an alliance between our people, then it will happen eventually. At least, that is what I told my mother before I shifted into my draka form and leapt from the balcony window to take flight.

I must know what landed in the desert seven days ago. I have been searching to no avail. Whatever fell from the sky, I feel its importance in my soul, and I will not rest until I discover what it was.

When I spoke with Noralla this morning, it was painfully obvious that she does not want this betrothal any more than I do. The tears in her eyes told me as much before she even opened her mouth. She has no desire to leave the Water Clan's territory to reside in the desert, just as I do not wish to take a mate I do not love, who does not love me.

The desert winds are strong this day as I extend my wings and slip into the current, leaving the castle and flying over the mesa toward the fields below. I dip low as I reach the river. A cool mist rises from the turbulent water to greet me, winding its way through an obstacle course of sharp rocks jutting up from the riverbed. Extending one limb, I skim the surface as I glide effortlessly over the vast, shimmering surface. My green eyes reflect in the crystalline liquid when I stare down at my draka form.

A deafening roar draws my attention away from my musings and back toward the castle. I shake my head in defiance at my father standing on my balcony, demanding my return.

He does not give pursuit because he lacks the conviction to chase after me. My father is well aware that the Water Princess and I are not fated like he and my mother were. If we were destined, this betrothal would be much simpler.

Though not all bonded pairs are fated to one another, I hoped to recognize the call of the fated bond when Noralla and I met. However, neither of us felt the pull when she arrived a few days ago with her twin brother, Llyr. We each looked down at our chests, searching the spot between our two beating hearts, but the glowing fate bond pattern never appeared.

When fated pairs meet, they recognize a pull to one another upon first sight. Then a glowing pattern emerges on the scales of their chests, directly between their hearts. It is called the fate mark. This is confirmation of the fated bonding, a sign one has found one's linaya—the fated one. The fate mark can take up to a year to appear, but it is always preceded by a knowing deep within. Noralla and I did not feel this when we saw each other.

Shaking my head, I turn away from the castle, refusing to allow my father's pleas to change my plans. The desert calls to me. An instinct within my soul fuels my desire to escape across the vast expanse of sand. As if fate is waiting for me within the desert sea, I go eagerly to find it.

The weight of my responsibilities can wait a little longer. I must answer this call. I have always trusted the fire that runs deep in my veins; right now, it leads me away from Noralla and toward the object that fell from the sky. If I find nothing, at least I will have tried.

Once Noralla and I are officially betrothed, I will no longer have the freedom to come and go as I please. I'll have cycles to spend by Noralla's side before my parents step down from rule. I need to cherish this final day of freedom before the future closes in around me.

Flapping my wings, I climb up over the steep plateau across the river. The sun's early rays peek above the horizon, scattering brilliant hues of red, orange, and yellow across the crimson desert sands. As my gaze sweeps the area below, I bank in a long, slow arc to head for the northern edge of our lands, toward Wind Clan territory.

I haven't patrolled our borders recently. If I'm lucky, Raidyn, Prince of the Wind Clan, will be somewhere nearby. It has been too long since I have had a good fight and he is always willing to oblige me.

As I dip and weave in and out of air currents, my gaze drifts over the endless expanse of the red desert plains. An ocean of sand undulates and flows beneath me like water as wisps of dust and mica sweep across the dunes. Towering rock formations stand proudly against the barren land.

Movement on the distant ground catches my eye, too far away to determine what it is. Dropping in altitude, I glide stealthily over the ground as I approach. I do not wish to scare what I've spotted. Not before I've had a chance to determine what moves about so freely beneath the bright glare of the sun. Most desert creatures wait until nightfall to emerge from their dens. The fact that this one does not, intrigues me.

I touch down behind a grouping of large boulders and shift into my two-legged form, making sure to remain down-wind to avoid detection. My crimson scales easily blend into the sand and rock as I conceal myself in the shadows and creep closer to investigate.

When I peek around a rock, I find the creature kneeling in the sand, facing away. The figure is clothed in strange coverings, with two arms and two legs like mine, but I do not immediately recognize the species. Until I am certain, I do not wish to make my presence known. Judging by the small stature, this could be an adolescent Drakarian or some other race entirely.

My people, the Drakarians, are capable of space travel, but since the Great Plague, we have adopted an isolationist policy, limiting our interactions with outsiders. After all, our Healers believe it was an off-world contagion that swept through our population. Because of this, all commerce with off-worlders takes place on the orbital station above Drakaria. No foreigners are allowed on the surface excepting a few Ambassadors of the Galactic Federation.

The figure leans down and grasps a handful of sand. The motion causes the clothing covering their torso to shift, revealing a pale, smooth expanse of flesh instead of scales. I notice no flying craft nearby. With no wings, I wonder how they traveled so far into the middle of the desert.

My gaze sweeps across the dunes and I wonder why they are alone. Perhaps they crashed and are seeking shelter. Once I determine which species I am dealing with, I will know whether this is friend or foe. Then I will either offer aid or leave them to their own devices.

Wind sweeps through the canyon and my nostrils flare. My eyes roll into the back of my head as the delicious feminine scent of this female is pulled deep into my lungs. A low rumbling growl of arousal reverberates through my chest.

She straightens as if alert then spins toward me. Her hood falls back, revealing smooth, pale flesh dotted with small, darkly pigmented spots across the bridge of her nose and cheeks. Long hair the color of flame hangs in loose waves around her shoulders.

I have never beheld a more beautiful female in my life.

I still and my jaw drops as my hearts pound. Primal possessiveness uncoils deep within me and my mind struggles to process what my body and soul have already embraced.

This strange female is my fated mate—my linaya.

A strange warmth fills my chest. When I glance down, I gape at the dimly glowing pattern the swirls across my scales, directly between my two hearts. Confirmation that what I feel for her is truth.

Raising a delicate hand to her brow to shield her lovely green eyes from the harsh sunlight, she squints in my direction. Caught, I quickly snap my jaw shut and give her a beaming smile like the enthralled male I now am.

All the stories I have heard are truth. Our meeting is everything I was told it would be. Happiness blooms in my chest. I have found she who is my destiny. Now, I need only to claim my mate and be claimed by her in return.

She is mine.

She stares at me and I'm surprised when recognition does not flash across her features. Does she not recognize the fated bond between us?

I open my mouth to speak but freeze when her gaze continues to travel over the rocks and sand nearby.

Realization hits me. Not every species is possessed of

acute vision like mine. We can see almost as well in the dark as in the light. She must have poor eyesight indeed to not notice me hidden here in the shadows.

Perhaps this is a blessing of sorts, as her distraction affords me time to study her before making my presence known. Strangely, I do not recognize her species. I rarely travel off-world, but enough that I should have encountered her kind on one of the many stations I've visited. However, I don't recall ever seeing a being like her among the Galactic Federation races.

Surely, I am mistaken. She cannot be mine. No Drakarian has ever found a fated mate in a race outside our own.

And yet, I am conflicted.

My body and soul urge me to claim her, but I am fearful because of her size. She is much smaller than a Drakarian female and I do not trust myself not to hurt her. Need burns through me like fire, but I push it back down. If she is my fated mate, I must treat her with great care. I cannot simply rush into a mating frenzy, as most do after recognizing their linaya.

No. The wiser decision would be to return to my people and report what I have found. I must bring back one of the Healers to assess this strange pull I feel toward this female. However much I desire her at this moment, I cannot simply claim her as I would another Drakarian. We are known throughout the quadrant for our strength, yet she appears rather fragile; I do not wish to hurt her.

I struggle to repress my need to claim her and retreat further into the shadows. As soon as I am out of sight, I quickly shift into my draka form and take to the sky, pumping my wings furiously to override the primal instincts inside me that insist I do not leave her. Although it is irrational, the prospect of another male claiming her instead fills me with anger.

Yes, I'm wise to retrieve a Healer. I do not trust myself to resist going into heat the moment her eyes meet mine and she, too, recognizes the bond between us.

A scream pierces the air, stopping my hearts. Alarm bursts through me and I twist, frantically flapping my wings as I race to return to her. My linaya is in danger.

CHAPTER 5

LILLIANA

Although I'm in the middle of the desert, I can't shake the feeling that someone is watching me. This is like a scene straight out of a horror story. The part where the plucky heroine—aka me—senses a disturbance in the air around her. All the while she's being stalked by some horrible, bloodthirsty monster.

Hysterical laughter bubbles up in my throat. I think the heat is getting to me.

Taking a deep breath, I allow my rational mind to overtake my overactive imagination. A while ago, I thought I saw a strange bird in the distant sky, but I haven't seen anything since. I've heard that excessive heat can cause you to hallucinate.

It's only been a week since our escape pod crashed on this barren rock of a planet. So far, we haven't come across any more of our people, but I'm sure we weren't the only ones to land here alive.

We can only survive on rations for so long before they run out. I kneel to gather another soil sample to take back to the rover. This planet is our new home, so we're going to need to settle down somewhere we can grow food. This sand looks like the desert sand of Earth, but I'm surprised to discover it's full of nutrients. I took the sample in the middle of a canyon, shielded from the harsh wind. This area could be just the shelter we're looking for.

The canyon is a step up from where our camp is set up now. We're sitting out in the open, exposed to the elements. It could be only a matter of time before a sandstorm hits, and I don't know that our makeshift shelters would offer enough protection.

Capping the sample tube, I stand. Tired from the heat of the sun relentlessly beating down overhead, I wipe the sweat from my brow and look longingly back at the rover. I can hardly wait to get back in the air-conditioned cab.

As I scan my surroundings, a disturbing thought occurs to me. I'm a botanist stranded on a desert planet. How crazy is that? Thank goodness we equipped each escape pod with survival seeds. When I became head botanist on the ship, that was one of my first suggestions to the Captain.

A few people on the council thought we were taking an unnecessary precaution, but I continued to push the idea after a horrible fire ravaged one of the biolabs on the ship last year. It wiped out almost half of our samples. I was afraid something similar could happen in the botanic lab and take out our entire seed inventory. The escape pods seemed like a great place to store extra seeds to be safe. I never imagined we'd need them in a situation like this. Like the rest of my crew, I got so comfortable with life on the ship, I never believed we'd ever encounter a problem we couldn't handle. I thought the seeds wouldn't be planted until we found a planet we all agreed upon to settle.

I shake my head in frustration. How wrong I was.

Now, as the only department head on our escape pod, I've been designated the leader. I'm not totally comfortable with my position yet, which is why I volunteered to scout for a new location alone. I need time to think and decide on our next step.

I'm not used to making survival decisions of this magnitude. This job entails so much more responsibility than simply making sure we grow enough food to keep our people fed. I never envied the Captain her position, but now I'm beginning to understand the stress she was under.

A soft scrape against the rocks behind me draws my attention and I turn toward the sound. Raising my hand to my brow, I shield my eyes from the sun as I try to determine the source of the noise. The angle of the sun casts long shadows between the canyon's large boulders. I stand completely still, listening for any indication that something is watching me.

A cool, dry breeze whips through the canyon and I release a heavy sigh of frustration. Why did the ship's builders design the escape pods as one-way tickets? Even if any of the other colony vessels escaped the space pirates who attacked us, we have no way to get back to them.

To make matters worse, we took a vote last night and the majority decided to destroy the distress beacon, just in case the pirates are still searching the area for us. The escape pods were meant to fit at least fifty people, but in all of the chaos, we launched at only half capacity. We may be the last humans left. We might never link up with other survivors—if there are any others, that is.

Closing my eyes, I can still picture the terrified expression of my neighbor, placing her palm against the glass and holding her daughter as the airlock sealed shut between us. I pray she made it off the ship alive.

Surely, other vessels made it. We cannot be the only ones.

Fate can't be that cruel, can it?

Yet even as I ask myself this question, my thoughts turn to Earth. We discovered recycling technologies, but not in time to save our planet. The generations before us poisoned our world beyond saving.

The escape pod was designed to be broken down for material to construct shelters. At least the technology that makes this possible is eco-friendly. We won't be harming this planet while we build our settlement and start a new life here.

Huffing a frustrated breath, I return to my work, kneeling in the soft, crimson sand to gather another sample.

A soft, skittering sound behind me draws my attention.

Is my imagination getting the best of me again?

The strange sound grows closer.

It's probably just the wind. Or maybe a cute, cuddly animal that wants to be my friend.

But my gut tells me this isn't the case. Dread trickles down my spine as I slowly spin to face the noise. My eyes widen. This thing is definitely not cuddly. A panicked cry escapes my throat as an enormous creature stalks toward me on four legs. Scales cover its entire body, shifting from orange to red and back again as it blends into the surrounding rocks like a chameleon with each step.

If I wasn't so scared, the higher-functioning part of my brain might be fascinated by such efficient camouflage. But the fight-or-flight part of my brain has taken charge as deep red eyes lock onto mine with a predatory gaze. Fear grips me in an iron vise, when I notice its snarling mouth full of shark-like teeth and lethal black claws. I reach for my blaster only to realize it's not on my belt. Cursing my luck, I remember that I left it in the rover behind me. Even if I sprint, I doubt I'll make it that far.

Slowly standing, I hold the creature's gaze as we carefully circle one another. It lowers its head as if readying to charge. If it's anything like a predator on Earth, maybe it will leave me alone if I try to appear bigger than I am. Straightening, I spread my arms wide as I face the beast, hoping and praying this strategy works.

It opens its mouth and releases a feral roar. Obviously, I'm only making it more angry.

Okay, bad idea. I need a new plan.

As my mind scrambles to come up with an idea, the predator decides for me as it charges forward.

I don't have any choice but to run.

Run or be eaten, my brain reminds me.

Panic beats at my chest. The fine grains of dirt are like quicksand beneath my boots as I struggle to race for the rover. I doubt I'll make it, but I don't have another choice. If I don't run, I'm dead anyway.

Something hard hits the back of my body, forcing the air from my lungs and sending me sprawling forward. Pain explodes across my skull when I land on a rock. I lift my head and the world tilts and spins around me, but I somehow manage to twist onto my back. The predator swipes one limb at me and I hold up my arm to shield my body. Massive claws rake across my forearm and I cry out as searing pain rips through me.

Warmth spreads through my body from the site, and my vision begins to blur. My mind floats in a strange haze of pure bliss. Somewhere in the back of my brain, I realize this must be the effect of a toxin from its claws coursing through me, but I'm far too gone to be concerned.

A low growl rumbles nearby, and it should be terrifying, but I find I don't really care. My vision blurs as darkness creeps in around the edges.

Wind swirls around me, kicking up dust and sand. A loud,

primal roar fills the air and I fall back. I blink up at a giant red dragon staring down at me, its beautiful crimson scales glinting beneath the sunlight.

"A real-life dragon," I barely manage to whisper before I close my eyes and fall away into darkness.

CHAPTER 6

VARUS

I remain in draka form as I rend flesh from bone with my sharp talons, ripping apart the sand tarkin that dared threaten my mate. Pitifully, it attempts to camouflage against the rocks, hoping I'll stop my assault. Perhaps that would confuse a lesser creature, but I am the apex predator here and I will not allow the tarkin to live after trying to kill what is mine.

Dealing another swift blow, I slam the creature against a large boulder. It releases a low, mournful sound as it crumples to the sand, the blood pooling beneath its form stains the earth black.

The sand tarkin draws in several ragged, shallow breaths as it lies dying. Normally, I'd end its suffering instantly. But this predator tried to harm my mate. It would have killed her if I had not been nearby and I cannot forgive such a transgression. I growl low in my throat. "You will suffer for trying to take that which is mine."

Turning away, I gaze down at her small form. "Are you all right?" I ask earnestly.

Green eyes fix me with an astounded stare as she barely manages to rasp, "A real-life dragon." Her head lolls back and she collapses against the sand.

Panicked, it takes me a moment to register the claw marks across her forearm. She must have passed out from the poison lacing the sand tarkin's claws. I have no idea how a female of her species will react to this toxin, so I must get her back to my Clan's Healer immediately.

Still in draka form, I reach out to scoop her up from the sand. I'm surprised by how light she is as I carefully curl my talons around her body, making sure I don't pierce her fragile skin. Fierce protectiveness grips me, and I hold her tiny form against my chest. The touch of her bare flesh against mine only strengthens the pull I feel toward this strange female.

Instinct beats inside my chest. Everything within me screams that she is mine.

Mine to protect, mine to possess, mine to keep, and mine alone to claim.

Dust and sand kick up around us as I extend and flap my wings to lift off. My hearts clench at the memory of her terror-filled cry.

How could I have left my fated one—my linaya?

She could have been killed. It's my fault she was alone and unprotected. Already, I have failed my mate. I can only pray she will forgive me once she wakes.

As we make our way across the desert plains, the wind grows stronger. My entire form shakes roughly for a moment before I slip into the current, billowing my wings to catch the warmer air in my sails. I head back toward the city and scan the area ahead, searching for any sign of a threat.

It occurs to me that my linaya may not be alone, but I saw

nothing to suggest there were others of her kind nearby. Perhaps she is an only survivor after all. I shudder to think what may have happened to her if I had not come along.

Something strange draws my attention off to the side. It is a solid, dark wall stretching across the horizon for several arcums in each direction, racing toward us at great speed.

My hearts stop and then begin pounding.

It's a sandstorm—a large one, at that. We don't have time to circumvent it. If I try to fly through the storm, I risk losing my mate and I will not leave her survival to chance.

I've seen what happens to Drakarians caught out in a sandstorm. Raw emotion stabs at my chest as I close my eyes and remember Prince Raidyn and his mother. Their bodies were battered and broken almost beyond recognition when my people finally found them. The Queen of the Wind Clan's love for her son is still spoken of in hushed whispers of admiration throughout the Fire kingdom. She was a brave female who chose the life of her son over her own that day.

I glance down at the unconscious form of my mate. We cannot risk facing the storm head-on; we will have to find shelter.

Frantic, I search for some kind of cover that could serve to shield us from the passing storm. Sandstorms can last for hours or even days.

I scan the horizon and notice a high plateau in the distance. My pulse pounds in my ears as I approach, sending a silent prayer to the Gods that we make it before the storm is upon us. If we do not, I will have to shield my mate with my body. I doubt I'd survive but I know that she, at least, would. And that is all that matters.

Flying closer, I notice several caves carved into the cliff wall. I search for one large enough to accommodate my draka form and deep enough to provide shelter from the wind and sand. I send another silent prayer to the Gods I cursed earlier this morning, asking for them to spare my mate.

Has ever a male been tested so early in a pairing?

I already failed to protect her once when I left her at the mercy of a predator, and I will not fail again. My vow.

When I reach the cliff face, a yawning cave mouth deep enough to shelter in from the sandstorm catches my attention. Hovering just outside the space, I peer into the darkness and see nothing. Just to be safe, I draw in a deep breath and then blow a long trail of flame, hoping to chase away or burn any occupants that might have scaled the steep terrain and claimed this cave already. I cannot defend my mate from predators in such a small, enclosed space. My draka form is at least five times larger than my two-legged form and she could be easily harmed if I'm not careful.

Satisfied when nothing stirs in the darkness, I carefully drift onto the small ledge just outside the entrance. As my claws grip the edge, a few chunks of rock crumble beneath my grasp and fall away, tumbling to the earth below.

Worry fills me as I look to my linaya.

My mate does not have wings. I will have to make certain she does not venture outside our shelter without me for fear that she might fall.

As soon as we're inside, I shift into my two-legged form and carry my still-unconscious female toward the back of the cave. Several crystals embedded in the walls cast a soft orange glow through the tunnel, lighting my way. This is fortunate since my mate does not seem to possess the ability to see well in the dark… or at all for that matter.

I shudder inwardly as I think back on how easily she missed me hiding in the shadows of the rocks earlier. I was downwind from her then and did not realize that another creature, such as the sand tarkin that attacked her, could use the same advantage to sneak up on her. I shake my head in frustration, then reach down and brush the hair back from her face, gently cupping her cheek as I whisper, "I vow that I will not fail you again, my linaya."

I hold her close to my chest while I explore the cave. A small pool shimmers near the back of the cavern—a fortunate find. We will not have to venture out for water if we're trapped in the cave for days. The rock floor warms beneath my feet as I approach the pool. It is not unusual to find warm springs in caves like this, but I wonder if the water is too hot for my mate. Her skin feels a bit cooler than mine, though that could be normal for her species.

I clench my jaw in frustration. There is so much I do not know about her, and I worry that I will be unable to care for her properly if she does not wake so I can ask about her needs.

Carefully, I lay her down on the floor. She is still asleep, affording me a chance to study her in greater detail. Her outer coverings are made of strange, coarse fabric I've never felt before. Nothing like the soft, silken robes my people wear when they choose to be clothed.

The top is sleeveless, revealing the entire length of her arms from her shoulders to her hands. The claw marks across her left forearm have stopped bleeding. I am surprised to notice that her blood dries red instead of black like my people and most species that occupy this quadrant of the galaxy.

Regardless of her strange features, the angry marks in her flesh must be cleaned if they are to heal without infection. Because I left the castle in draka form, I have no clothing, so I must use some of hers to clean her wounds. I wonder if her people can shift forms. Many sentient species can, but surely if she could, she would have done so while under attack from the sand tarkin.

I study her legs and notice the fabric clings to her form

like a second skin before tucking into a pair of boots. I remove the coverings from her feet then dip my hands beneath the waistband of her pants and gently roll them down her hips and legs, removing them from her body. I do the same with her upper coverings, baring her form to my gaze as I check her for further injury.

Her pale, creamy flesh is covered with a scattering of small, darkly pigmented spots. I'm aghast to find that she lacks any sort of protective scales as I run my hands over her soft skin.

She is very different from a Drakarian female. Instead of a flat expanse of muscle across her chest, two large, soft mounds rise above her hearts. I wonder what these are for. I have heard some species nurse their young after giving live birth. Perhaps that is the case for her kind. She wears a strange band of cloth across them. Another strip of fabric covers her pelvic area, concealing her feminine place.

Despite my curiosity, I do not dare remove either piece of clothing to inspect her further, suspecting her species might consider such an action indecent.

She may be my mate, but she has not permitted me to touch her intimately. In the back of my mind, I wonder if she ever will once she realizes that I abandoned her in the desert, leaving her vulnerable to attack by the sand tarkin.

A Drakarian female would never forgive such a careless act of negligence.

Her skin reminds me of the petals of the inora flower. Soft and delicate, this flower is so fragile that even the slightest touch can bruise it. I'm careful as I skim the tips of my calloused fingers across her body to check her for injury, noting the mottled discoloration of her chest and abdomen that I surmise may be bruising.

What could have harmed her in this way? These marks

were not left by the sand tarkin. They claw and bite their prey, but do not beat them.

I bite back a snarl at the thought of another harming my mate. My mind recalls the image of fire trailing across the sky and suddenly everything falls into place. My mate fell from the stars. Since I noticed no wreckage near where I found her, I'm not sure how she survived.

My mouth drifts open as I eye her form. What if she is alone? The sole survivor of a terrible crash? Why else would she be wandering the desert all by herself and unprotected?

My hand trails up her body and I circle my fingers around her wrist, feeling the delicate bones beneath her skin. Gently, I cup her cheek and turn her face toward mine.

She is fragile, my mate. I realize I will have to take great care to not harm her accidentally during our mating, if she ever allows such a thing.

Even if she does not, it is my duty to care for her, and I will do so gladly.

My hearts clench as she turns her head into my palm and a soft sigh escapes her. She nestles against my body and I gently extend my wings forward to encircle her.

She instinctively turns to me for comfort. Unbearable fear threatens to consume me. Already, the mate bond has firmly anchored in my soul and my hearts simultaneously plummet and soar. I am terrified to fail in protecting such a delicate female and yet, happy beyond measure that I have found she who is mine.

Lifting her small hand, I study the blunted claws that tip her fingers. She sighs again and I gasp as I notice her flat, white teeth, devoid of sharp edges. How will she eat? Will I have to chew her food for her like a newly hatched fledgling?

With a heavy sigh, I shake my head in frustration.

Couldn't the Gods at least have seen fit to give my mate wings so she could fly from danger? How could the Gods create such a defenseless species? How has my mate's race managed to survive? They must hail from a safe, temperate planet to have evolved with no natural defenses.

Balling the fabric once covering her torso in one hand, I approach the water. I will use this material to clean her wounds, then search for caza root, which shouldn't be difficult to find. This plant thrives in dark spaces and caves are ideal growing spots. The root can disinfect her wounds—I hope.

I'm glad I spent so much time with Healer Ranas of the Earth Clan, one of the most skilled Healers among his people. He has taught me many things, among them how to find medicinal plants.

Little did I know that I would need his teachings to heal my mate's injury. I am thankful at this moment, that I have always been a curious male, or else I never would have thought to study under Ranas.

Dragging the wet cloth gently across her injured skin, I am glad that at least one thing is going right for me this day. I should have no problem locating the healing roots my mate requires.

When I'm satisfied that her wounds are clean, I study her sleeping form. She appears so vulnerable that I am loath to leave her in such a helpless state, but I have no choice. Though the winds have died down a bit, the sandstorm is still raging.

I cannot leave her injuries untreated. Especially since I do not know how long we will be trapped here.

CHAPTER 7

LILLIANA

Awareness slowly trickles back into my mind at the sound of rushing wind. My eyes snap open to face dark, uneven, red stone walls. The smell of damp earth fills my nostrils, and a soft orange glow illuminates the space. I blink in wonder when I realize the light is emanating from strange crystals embedded within the rock. They cast just enough light that I'm able to see clearly as my vision slowly adjusts.

I must be in a cave, but how did I get here?

I sit up and then gasp when I realize I'm naked, except for my bra and underwear. Thank goodness I'm at least still wearing those. How did I lose my clothes?

My pants are folded neatly beside me, while my top is bunched up, wet, and stained pink with blood. I lift my arm and a sharp sting of pain draws my attention to deep claw marks on my skin. A myriad of images fill my mind as my memory returns. A small shudder runs through my body when I recall the large predator that attacked me.

I remember feeling faint, but not much after that. I certainly don't have any memory of finding this shelter or cleaning my wounds.

Maybe someone from our campsite found me—hopefully, one of my friends or Talia's brother Milo. He's like a brother to me also, so I'd feel a little less self-conscious if one of them dragged me here and undressed me.

The fleeting memory of hitting my head returns. I gasp as the image of a terrifying red dragon fills my mind. I reach up and run my hands through my hair, checking my skull for any sign of injury.

Oh, my Stars! Did I really see a dragon?

Is that why I'm here—I ran and hid in this cave?

I must be going crazy from dehydration. Or maybe the blow to my head caused me to hallucinate. Then again, I realize we *are* on an alien world. Despite how similar the environment may appear, this certainly isn't Earth. Anything is possible here.

Drawing in a deep, steadying breath, I attempt to calm myself by taking stock of my situation. It's safe to say that I'm in a cave, sheltered from whatever rages beyond these walls. The wind howls outside, covering the cavern mouth in a thick cloud of swirling dust. Red sand gathers in a small pile just inside the entrance. So, as I suspected, the desert is plagued by sandstorms.

Panic races through me when I think of my friends at the campsite. Skye, Anna, Talia, Milo, and the rest of our crew. Stars, I hope they're all right.

We talked about the possibility of sandstorms, at least, before I left. Our consensus was that if one came along, we'd take shelter in the least damaged part of the escape pod. It isn't very big, but it could fit everyone in a worst-case scenario.

They're smart, and I'm sure they took shelter before the

storm hit. I have to believe this or else I'll go crazy with worry. And right now, I need to focus on figuring out where I am and how I got here so I can get back to my people after the storm passes.

Since it isn't safe to venture outside now, I turn toward the back of the cave and notice the rippling reflections along the rock wall. I breathe a small sigh of relief when I realize a large pool of water is scattering the light. At least one thing is going well today. As long as the water isn't contaminated, I won't die of dehydration while I'm here.

Cautiously, I explore the cave, peering around every large rock and boulder, searching for any tunnels or openings— any indication that I'm not alone. The stone floor is hard and offers no clues like footprints and such to indicate how I got here and whether I'm safe. The last thing I want is to run into another predator. After a thorough search, I find nothing, but I still can't remember how I ended up here.

Closing my eyes, I struggle to focus on the last thing I remember before I passed out. Panic coils tightly in my chest as the blood-curdling image of the dragon resurfaces. As much as I wish I did, I don't think I imagined the encounter. I'm pretty sure the beast was real. So where is it now?

What if this dragon is just like the fairy tales—it only eats virgins?

Oh Stars, if it does, I'm doomed. Twenty-three years old and I'm going to die a virgin. On a desert planet. In the middle of nowhere.

Anxiety spirals through me, filling my mind with the terrifying image of being ripped apart by a blood-thirsty dragon. This just keeps getting worse by the minute.

I knew I should have gone on that date with Ryan. Why didn't I? Oh yeah, that's right; he was the resident lady's man on deck. However, if I'd just let down my walls and relaxed a bit, maybe I would have found a boyfriend by now, formed at least one close relationship, instead of being alone, single, and still a virgin. Aka: tempting dragon snack.

But no, I just had to be a hopeless romantic. Always lost in the romance novels I borrowed from the ship's library and dreaming of the perfect man that doesn't exist in real life.

With a heavy sigh of frustration, I gather my clothes and quickly pull them back on. I can't change the past and now, I'm looking at the possibility of remaining single forever. Assuming I don't get eaten by a dragon.

Out of the twenty-five refugees on the escape pod, only five are men. One of them is old enough to be my father, one is a complete creep, another is a womanizer, one is only interested in men, and the last is my best friend's brother. If we don't find any other survivors, I'm going to die alone.

My mind starts to spiral again, and I force myself to take another deep, calming breath. One thing at a time. First, I need to figure out where I am in relation to the rover. If I can find the rover, then I can reach my people. Who, hopefully, have not died in a sandstorm or been eaten by a dragon.

I shake my head, irritated. I really need to get ahold of myself and focus. Imagining worst-case scenarios isn't doing me any good.

I'm just about to put on my boots when a great rush of air fills the cave with dust and sand, nearly knocking me over. I squeeze my eyes shut against the grit as I cough out the fine particles trying to invade my lungs. I look up toward the cave mouth and my jaw drops when I catch sight of a naked man walking toward me.

Correction: A naked *alien* man walking toward me.

Covered from head to toe in deep-crimson scales, with a long, tapered tail and lethal dark claws tipping each of his five fingers and toes, he bares his teeth, revealing two rows of enormous, sharp fangs. A pair of twisted, onyx horns frame his long, red hair, drawing my attention to his face.

He holds something out to me. I'm frozen in shock as his green, vertically slit pupils contract then expand. He opens his mouth and makes a series of harsh, guttural noises.

A terrified scream erupts from my throat as I realize I'm about to be eaten.

CHAPTER 8

VARUS

S uccessful in my hunt for the caza root, I return triumphantly to the cave. I hope my mate will be impressed by my skill in the arts of healing.

To my surprise, she is already awake and standing before me. She stares up at me with luminous, deep-green eyes. I am so happy that she is well enough to stand, I smile at her as I hold out the caza root in offering.

"Here, my mate," I tell her as my chest puffs out with pride. "I have retrieved this healing root for your wounds."

I'm glad she is no longer unconscious so that I can show her what a capable male I am. I was able to gather this for her and now, I will treat her injuries with as much skill as any Healer.

Her features twist into a mask of horror and she screams.

I spin, terrified that perhaps a predator may have snuck up behind me, trying to claim our cave as his. I growl low in warning. Whatever frightens her, I will kill it. I wait a moment for the threat to make its presence known but sense nothing.

Curious, I turn back to her. "What is it? What did you see? Where is the danger? Tell me and I shall end its life. I will protect you, my mate."

I take a step toward her. Panic coils tightly in my chest when she releases another feral cry of terror. I spin back toward the cave entrance, flaring my wings wide to shield her as I crouch into a defensive position, ready to attack anything that dares to enter our cavern.

Something bumps the back of my spine and her foot steps on the tip of my tail.

I quickly curl it around to my side, out of her way. Oh Gods, something has driven her to panic and stumble into me.

I turn back to reassure her. "Do not fear, my linaya. I will protect you—" I stop abruptly when she rushes toward me.

Surprised and elated that she is already racing into my arms, I spread them wide to receive her. This is excellent. I've heard Drakarian females rush into a male's arms, practically attacking him, when they are ready to mate. Driven mad with the desire of their heat cycle, they go into a mating frenzy, which I've heard can last for days.

Drawing in a deep breath, I ready myself to please my mate. I have learned all that I can of the art of pleasuring a female from speaking with the mated Drakarian guards at the castle. I'm hoping she will be particularly aroused when I bind her wrists together with my tail then clamp my teeth around her neck with just enough pressure to hold her still and increase her anticipation as I enter her channel.

My stav begins to lengthen and throb against the inside of my mating pouch, ready to extend as soon as she opens her thighs to receive me.

Lust-driven thoughts of her biting my neck in return fill

my mind. Lost in my fantasy, I barely manage to duck in time to avoid her arm swinging at me. I'm so stunned, I don't move as she swipes at me again. The weak hit bounces off my scales and she draws back her hand, shaking it back and forth as she hisses in pain.

I cock my head to the side in confusion. "Why are you trying to attack me? Is this some sort of mating ritual among your people?" I have heard of this practice among other species. Perhaps hers is the same.

Cautiously, I move closer and she strikes me again. I deflect her blows effortlessly. She pulls back and begins to circle me, baring her teeth.

"If this is a test of strength, I believe I have proven I am strong enough to protect you and our future fledglings. Assuming we are compatible in that way."

I grin, hoping she will be impressed by my answer. I want her to know I am already thinking of our future. I have heard that females are attracted to males who speak of fledglings early in the mating.

"If you think I'm going down without a fight, you're wrong, you big, ugly… lizard man!"

My jaw drops as I stare at her, aghast. *"Lizard man?* What is that?" I look down at my figure. "I am Drakarian."

"You want to growl at me?" she yells. "I can growl, too!"

And with that, she bares her flat, white teeth again and begins making pitiful growling sounds, reminiscent of adolescent fledglings before their voices drop.

"I am not growling at you," I protest, incredulous. "I am speaking."

She growls again and the realization hits me. She must not have a translator chip. She doesn't understand what I'm saying.

She makes another swipe with her blunt claws.

I grit my teeth in frustration. This will not do. I cannot

have my linaya afraid of me when all I want to do is protect her.

Why doesn't her species have translator chips? From what sort of primitive planet does she hail?

Both these questions and more run through my mind. Sighing heavily, I realize what I must do. It will not be easy. She is already afraid of me and I am loath to worsen her fears, but I have no choice.

I run my hand roughly through my hair then cautiously move toward her. She is my fated mate, so she should be able to hear my thoughts when transmitted through touch. I only hope I can reach out to the mind of a female of a different species.

With her hands balled into fists before her chest, she narrows her eyes, watching me warily as I approach. "Stay back," she grits through her flat, white teeth. "I mean it."

I hate that she fears me when I am the one she should trust most. We are fated to be together. Does she not feel the pull of the bond? A glance at her chest heightens my concern. I do not see a glow across her skin in the fated mark pattern. Perhaps she does not recognize our connection, or her species is incapable of sensing the bond.

With each step I take toward her, she steps further back, until she is nearing the cave entrance and the cliff edge. I hold my hands out in a placating gesture. "Please," I plead in a soft voice. "I'm not trying to hurt you. I swear."

My words and gestures do nothing to reassure her as she keeps backing toward the edge without knowledge of what lies beyond. My hearts stop in horror as visions of her accidentally tripping and falling into the storm and off the cliff fill my mind.

I just discovered my fated mate—I refuse to lose her to a misunderstanding. On the same day that I found her, no less.

Drawing in a deep breath, I rush forward and scoop her

into my arms, pulling her back into the cave and away from the dangerous cliff.

She flails wildly in my grasp, kicking, hitting, and biting at me. Her smooth, flat teeth latch onto my arm and a panicked thought flits through me that she may not be as defenseless as she seems. After all, many creatures in the desert appear harmless until they attack you, like the adorable sorana with its wide eyes and fluffy tuft of orange fur. She might carry a paralyzing agent or deadly venom in her saliva.

But I refuse to let her go and risk her running off the cliff edge and tumbling to her death. Holding on tightly, I close my eyes to steady my breathing, waiting for the poisonous toxin to kick in and end me.

"If I am going to die," I tell her, "Let it be protecting you, my cherished one."

She stills, then unclamps her jaw from my arm and peers up at me with wide eyes. "I can understand you."

A smile tugs at my lips. "Because I am touching you. You do not seem to have a translator chip. Unless," I run my hand behind her ear, feeling for the small device, "it has been damaged somehow."

She bats my hand away. "What's a translator chip?"

I blink at her, stunned. For one so defenseless, she is very brave to strike a Drakarian warrior. My female is fierce, and I admire this in her. It concerns me, however, that she does not have a chip. "Your species must be very primitive indeed."

The words escape my mouth before I even realize I've spoken them aloud.

"Primitive?" She gestures to the space around us as she glares up at me. "Who are you to talk? *You* live in a cave."

Despite my best attempt to hold it in, a bellowing laugh escapes me.

She narrows her eyes. If that is her angry face, I find it rather adorable. "What's so funny?"

I arch a teasing brow. "I'll have you know that I do not—and have never—lived in a cave."

"Then why are we here?"

I gesture to the storm raging outside. "A sandstorm was approaching, and we needed shelter. This was the closest place."

"Let me go," she commands.

"Fine, but if we are to communicate, we must remain touching."

With a slight huff, she nods, and I loosen my grip on her forearm.

"I am Varus," I place a hand on my chest. "What is your name?"

"I'm Lilliana. Lilly for short," she adds.

"Lilliana," I repeat her name softly. It is lovely, just like her.

I am a lost male indeed.

CHAPTER 9

VARUS

Lilliana. Such a strange, yet beautiful name. I long to know everything about her. "Where do you come from?"

She lowers her gaze. "Earth," she replies, and I cannot help but notice the sadness that steals across her features. Inhaling deeply, she lifts her green eyes back to mine. "What's the name of this planet?"

"Drakaria." I cock my head to the side. "Have you not heard of my people?"

"No, I haven't," she replies, stunning me. She must be from a very distant and remote place indeed to not know of Drakarians, for my people are among the most feared in the quadrant.

Standing in such close proximity, my gaze travels down her form. Perhaps I was wrong. Maybe her species *does* possess natural defenses, but she has not yet grown into them. She is much smaller than Drakarian females. "You are rather small. Your fangs are flat, and your claws are blunted. Are you fully matured?"

Her jaw drops. "What kind of question is that? Yes, I'm mature. I'll have you know I'm average height for my... species. And," she looks down at her hands, "my *claws*," she accentuates the word, "are normal for my people. We don't have fangs—we have teeth."

This news is very disconcerting. My concerns for her safety have now grown exponentially. I'd hoped she would at least grow a few more tarems in height so she would not be so much smaller than my people.

She looks down at my hand on her arm. "So, this is how your species communicate?"

"Some of us," I reply with a half-truth. I do not tell her that this is how fated mates communicate. She thinks I am ugly; she will not be pleased to learn that we are fated to one another just yet. "Tell me. How did you come to be in the desert?"

"Our ship was attacked by pirates," she replies. "We evacuated on an escape pod and landed here."

I cock my head to the side. "We? Are there more of you?"

She nods. "Twenty-five."

Alarm bursts through me as I dart another glance toward the storm. If her people were caught in this storm, they are likely dead. "Where is the rest of your crew?"

"Not far from where you found me," she answers. "It was less than an hour's drive in the rover from our campsite."

With a slight clench of my jaw, I struggle to understand this unit of time she has given me as my translator tries to equate the word to something familiar.

As if sensing my confusion, she offers, "It wasn't very far."

I meet her eyes evenly and ask the most important question. "Did they have adequate shelter?"

"Yes. A large part of the escape pod remained undamaged.

They could hold up in there if a storm came along." She also glances toward the entrance and the storm outside. "I guess I was right about this place," she mutters, more to herself than to me.

"About what?" I ask, curious to understand.

"I'm a botanist, so I studied many different terrains on my former home world. And this place," she gestures out toward the desert, "is similar to the desert plains of my planet. I figured there was a strong possibility that sandstorms like this might hit, so I had already suggested to my crew that we use the escape pod as a shelter."

I blink several times, processing. She is as brilliant as she is beautiful. The Gods have blessed me with such a clever mate.

"That was wise," I tell her and watch as she straightens slightly with pride. "To have planned for such an event based on your cumulative experiences."

She smiles and it is the most beautiful expression I have ever seen.

"Thanks." She lifts her shoulders toward her ears in a strange gesture. "I got a bit of flak from one of the guys for that idea. He accused me of inciting panic by speculating about a disaster."

I frown. It seems the males of her species are not as smart as the females. "His rebuke of your foresight was foolish," I state firmly. "A smart leader must always think ahead."

Her smile brightens even more, and I am completely enthralled. Her cheeks begin to redden under my gaze, and I wonder if this is the first sign of the mating flush. Our females blush when preparing to go into heat. Her expressive green eyes stare deep into mine and I take the chance to scoot closer to her, satisfied when she does not retreat.

Her gaze travels down my form, pausing a moment at the slit of my mating pouch and the muscles defining my arms and legs. She seems to be appraising me like a Drakarian female, so I tilt up my chin and puff my chest out with pride, hoping she will find me appealing, rather than ugly as she called me earlier. She purses her lips as her cheeks darken. "Can you please cover up?"

My chest deflates. "What?"

"You're naked. I don't need to see all that." She gestures to the length of my body with her hand. "Put some clothes on."

I blink several times in shock. My wounded pride will never recover from this devastating blow. I've always considered myself rather handsome. At least, that's what my mother always told me, as did the dozens of females who vied for my hand before my parents finally settled on Noralla to unite our people with the Water Clan.

But I suppose they could have been lying. After all, I am my mother's only son—now, her only child—so I must be perfect in her eyes for that reason alone. And the other females just want my status and title.

I am a fool. An ugly fool.

"I do not have any clothes," I tell her dryly.

Her mouth drifts open. "Why not?"

My brow furrows, confounded. "Do you mean to say that your people always wear coverings?"

Her jaw drops. "Yours don't?"

I shake my head.

"Oh Stars, I've stumbled upon some alien nudist colony," she grumbles to herself.

"Alien nudist colony?" I ask incredulously. "Are your people ashamed of your bodies? You did not look so terrible without your clothing."

She gasps and then glares at me accusingly. "*You* undressed me?"

I shoot her an incredulous look. "Of course, I did. How else was I supposed to check you for injury?"

"What. The. Hell." She runs a hand through her long, thick red hair and then shakes her head in disbelief. After a moment, she lifts her gaze to mine. "All right. I suppose if nudity isn't a big deal to your people, you probably didn't know any better. Even though," she narrows her eyes, "you violated my privacy."

I inhale sharply. "You believe I violated you?" I gawk at her as my stomach twists into a violent knot at the idea. "I would never do such a thing."

Her brow furrows slightly. "All right. I guess you look shocked enough that I believe you. In any case, we have bigger fish to fry."

I cock my head to the side. "This phrase is not translating correctly. Are you trying to tell me you are hungry?"

She laughs a moment before her expression sobers and I wish she would laugh again. It was a beautiful sound.

"No, that's not what I mean." She gestures to the cave mouth. "There's probably a huge, bloodthirsty, monstrous dragon outside, flying around and waiting to eat us."

I frown in confusion. "What is a dragon? Do you refer to the animal that attacked you? I killed it. It will no longer trouble you. My vow."

Her jaw drops as she stares at me with eyes full of wonder. "You killed it?"

She appears awed by my battle prowess, so I tip my chin higher then dip my head in a subtle nod while discreetly flexing my biceps.

"Yes. It is dead. By my hand," I add, proud that she is so easily impressed by such a simple kill. Perhaps I should slay a fiercer beast for her next meal to further prove my worth.

"I can't believe you killed the dragon. You saved me! That's amazing! I'm so glad I met you!"

I grin. This is suddenly going rather well, I think.

She extends one arm up and away from her body as far as

she can while still holding onto me with the other so we can communicate.

"It was massive." Her eyes grow big. "With huge wings and sharp claws and scales and long, vicious fangs and that spiked tail and…"

My hearts sink as she continues describing me in my draka form.

"It was one of the meanest, ugliest-looking monsters I've ever seen! I can't believe you killed it!"

Oh… it's definitely dead now. And by that, I mean from grievously injured pride. A mortal wound for any warrior looking to impress his mate.

"It is assuredly dead," I agree as I lower my gaze to the floor. My fated mate thinks I am hideous. I am going to die old and alone.

She pokes at one of the claw wounds on her arm and winces slightly.

Even if she does not desire me, I can at least be a good mate and care for her. "Here." I hold out the roots I have gathered. "I have brought something to heal your wounds."

She takes it from my hand, biting her lower lip as she studies it curiously. "What am I supposed to do with this? Eat it?"

I gasp and quickly take it back from her. "You cannot eat that. It will make you sick."

"How was I supposed to know that?" She gives me a withering look. "Okay, genius, what do I do with it, then?"

Genius? She believes I am exceptionally smart? This is good. Many females have chosen their mates based on intellect alone. I should know—my grandparents met that way. My grandfather is not a handsome male by any measure, but my grandmother is stunningly beautiful. She said it was his sharp and intelligent mind that attracted her.

This is something I can work with. My hearts soar. All is not lost.

I smile. "Please, sit, so I may treat your wound."

She takes a seat on the floor, staring up at me expectantly.

Popping one of the caza roots into my mouth, I begin chewing it thoroughly.

"I thought you weren't supposed to eat it?"

I hold up a hand, gesturing for her to wait patiently while I chew the medicine into a fine paste. When I'm satisfied with the consistency, I spit the ball into my free hand and reach for her wound.

She jerks away violently. "What the hell are you doing?"

Even as she pulls away, it doesn't escape me that she's still holding my other arm firmly so that we can communicate. "I'm trying to treat your wound."

"I don't think so." Her eyes are wide as I chase her in a circle.

"You need caza root to make sure your wound does not become infected."

We continue to spin in a circle. I struggle to catch her flailing, injured arm. She twists away from me.

"It most certainly will become infected if you slather it with alien spit," she retorts. "I would rather take a chance eating the root than having you place your paste on me."

"Alien spit? This is a medicinal paste," I correct her. "Now, stop moving and stay still so I can treat you."

"No way!"

A low growl of frustration rumbles up from my throat. "I will not have you dying of infection on my watch, female."

She goes still and all the color drains from her face. "The germs are that bad here?"

Recognizing the opportunity that has been presented to me, I nod. "Yes."

It is yet another half-truth, but I comfort myself with the

knowledge that it is not a complete lie. And… it is for her own good. Only the Gods know, what would be a simple fever for my kind might be deadly to hers.

I must be diligent in attending to her needs.

She glares up at me. If this isn't a test from the gods, then I don't know what is.

Reluctantly, she holds out her arm and allows me to apply the medicinal paste, all the while wrinkling her nose and grimacing. If she feels so strongly about my saliva, I cannot imagine the disgust she would feel if I ever brought up the idea of mating.

With a heavy sigh, I imagine myself alone in my chambers, staring up at the ceiling until the end of my days. I will die alone, never knowing the pleasures of sharing my bed with a mate.

After I finish applying the paste, she studies the wound a moment then looks up at me. "So… what do you do? Are you a doctor?"

"Doctor?"

"Um… you know, healing people and such?"

"Ah," I reply, finally understanding. "You mean a Healer."

She nods.

"No, I am not a Healer."

"Well then, what do you do?"

I'm about to tell her I'm the Prince of the Fire Clan, but luckily catch myself before the words leave my mouth. I want to know if it is possible for my fated one to like me for who I am instead of my status among my people. Unable to think of a quick lie, I reply a bit awkwardly. "I… don't really do anything."

This is actually quite close to truth. Until I am king, my duties are light and my days are often filled with boredom.

"So, you're unemployed?" she asks a bit hesitantly.

Offended by her tone, I tilt up my chin. "Like all members

of my Clan, I am a warrior." Narrowing my eyes, I tip my head to the side as I regard her. "What do you do?"

"I'm a botanist," she answers, studying one of the caza roots intensely. "And I have the perfect name for it."

"How so?"

"Well, Lilliana sounds like a lily."

"What is a lily?"

"A beautiful flower on my home world—Earth."

My gaze drifts to her petal-soft skin. The name does suit her well. She is as beautiful and delicate as a flower. However, I am sorry that fate has seen fit to bring her to my Clan. A botanist in a desert is less than ideal. She would have been better suited to mate a member of the Earth Clan, living in their rich territory teeming with vegetation.

Yet, even as this thought enters my mind, fierce possessiveness rushes through me. She is mine and I cannot bear the thought of her with another. I force myself to stifle the growl threatening to rise in my throat. I study her hand on my arm. She is growing accustomed to me, I think. Perhaps, in time, she will even come to like me.

Regardless, I am unwilling to give her up to a member of the Earth Clan. I will endeavor to be the best mate that I can so that, hopefully, it will make up for that fact that choosing a life with me means living in the Fire Clan territory.

Earth. The name of her home world drifts through my mind. Strange that her people named their planet after dirt. "The name of your planet is unfamiliar to me. Is your race part of the Galactic Federation of Planets?"

Her brow wrinkles. "What's that?"

Her question stuns me. This is worse than I thought. I wonder if she comes from a Z class world—surely not.

She elaborates. "My crew's colony ships were the first spacecraft my species ever designed for deep space travel. Prior to our mission, we'd never left our planetary system."

My mouth drifts open. It is as I feared. Earth is a Z class planet in the infancy of space exploration. "How many ships were traveling with yours?"

She sighs. "The armada was made up of several large colony vessels. We were attacked by pirates. We tried to lose them in an asteroid field but took too much damage. My crew had to abandon ship." Her eyes brighten with tears, but she blinks them back. "A lot of people died. I'm not even sure how many of us made it—aside from us twenty-five in the escape pod."

"Do you need help to return to your home world?" I ask reluctantly. I would not truly wish for her to leave, but I will not force her to stay here either. It is not our way. The female makes the decision to either accept or reject a male interested in becoming her mate.

She shakes her head sadly. "We are the last of our race. We had to leave our planet because the generations before us... poisoned our world beyond saving."

It must be terrible to lose one's home, but I cannot deny the relief that washes through me at her answer. It would have been difficult, if not impossible, to let her go if she had somewhere to return to.

"I am sorry about your world, Lilly." The lie burns like bitter acid on my tongue for it is a half-truth. I truly feel saddened that she lost her home, but I am glad she has no reason to leave Drakaria either.

She gives me a faint smile. "Thank you, Varus. And... thank you for saving me from that awful creature."

With a heavy sigh, I nod, inwardly cringing at the words she chooses to refer to my draka form.

CHAPTER 10

LILLIANA

I dart a glance toward the cave entrance. The wind appears to have died down a bit. Long shadows stretch over the cliffside as the sun begins to set. If I want to reach my people before nightfall, I need to leave soon.

"The storm seems to be letting up, don't you think?"

Varus glances to the exit. "No. This is simply a lull."

"Well… how long do these sandstorms normally last? How long do you think we'll be here?"

"It could be several days."

My jaw drops. "Several days?" He nods. "But I can't stay gone that long. I need to get back to my people. Besides, how are we supposed to survive in this cave for days? What about food and water?"

He frowns. "The pool at the back of the cave is safe to drink from. And food? I doubt we will be here longer than a week."

"A week without food?" I ask incredulously.

He cocks his head to the side. "How often does your species require nourishment?"

"I don't know about your people, but mine eat every day, more than once daily, even."

His brows shoot up, nearly disappearing into his hairline as unmistakable panic warps his features. "Do not worry. I will go hunting for you." His gaze darts again to the entrance and the storm outside. "Now, while the storm is still calm."

I hate to ask him to take that risk for me. I'm about to offer my help when he cuts me off.

"Do you think you can survive alone for a short period of time while I gather sustenance?" he asks in a serious tone.

My mouth drifts open, my expression frozen somewhere between shock and indignation. "Of course, I can survive on my own," I huff. "I'm not helpless, you know."

He says nothing, but the way he arches his brow tells me he doesn't entirely agree. His gaze travels discreetly down my form and the memory of his comments about my blunt claws and flat teeth returns.

He, on the other hand, looks like an apex predator with his lethal claws, sharp fangs, and strong, muscular build. I guess I can understand why he's concerned about my safety. As this thought crosses my mind, I remember the blood-thirsty dragon and suddenly worry about what other predators may be lurking on this world.

He clears his throat, pulling me back from my dark thoughts. "If the winds pick up again, your skin will not protect you from the sand like my scales protect me. And if we run into any more predators, I would be torn between defending you and defeating our enemy and—"

I roll my eyes. He doesn't have to remind me of how pitiful he thinks I am. I lift my hands in mock surrender. "Alright, alright, I get it. You think I'm weak and will only slow you down—fine. I promise I'll stay here while you go get food."

Images of the scary dragon resurface in my mind. I grip his forearm and meet his eyes anxiously.

"Please, be careful while you're out there. Promise me you'll come back, alright?"

CHAPTER 11

VARUS

My ears perk up at her words. She is asking me to promise to return to her; not to leave her. A faint smile curves my lips. It seems we are already bonding. Perhaps some part of her feels the pull of the fate bond like I do. Already, she is expressing territorial tendencies as a Drakarian female would. She is probably worried I might seek out another female. I would never do such a thing, but she does not know that.

My hearts soar at the thought that her instincts have been triggered. She already considers me hers, demanding that I return to her side. I dip my chin in a subtle nod to my mate. "I vow that I will return to you."

She smiles brightly. "I'll be here waiting for you."

I cannot believe I ever found her appearance strange; she is the most beautiful female I have ever seen. Has any male ever been so blessed as I to have such an attractive mate?

I turn to leave but then spin back to face her. Every instinct demands that I stay by her side, but she needs food.

To be a good mate to her, I need to provide for her needs. Fierce protectiveness rushes through me and I take both her hands in mine, relishing the touch of her petal-soft skin. "Please, stay inside the cave. It is dangerous to venture too close to the edge of the entrance. There is a sharp drop below. If you are thirsty or need to bathe, the water in the pool is safe."

She tightens her grip on my forearm slightly and her luminous green eyes meet mine. "Alright. I got it, don't worry. I'll be waiting here for when you return."

I can only describe this wonderful feeling in my chest as pure joy. I have not even left, and she can hardly wait for my return. We are already bonding, it seems. The mated guards in my castle told me that a mated pair cannot stand to be apart during the initial days of the bond. I am already feeling this pull, but now it seems that she is as well.

Even as happiness blooms inside me, my shoulders sag when I remember how fearful she is of my draka form.

"Move to the back of the cave where it is safe from the winds, in case they worsen. I will return shortly with food."

She nods and I wait until she heads for the back of the cave so that she does not see me transform into my "monster" form. Eventually, I must tell her the truth of what I am, but for now, we've made great progress and I do not want to ruin it.

She already trusts me enough to allow me to prove that I can hunt and gather for her. Most female Drakarians pride themselves on their independence, only allowing a male to provide for them when they are ready to mate.

I inhale sharply. Perhaps she is preparing to nest. Maybe the fate bond has triggered this desire within her. Warmth fills my entire body at the memory of the deep-crimson flush of her cheeks only moments ago. Perhaps when I come back, she will insist upon our first mating.

Though, I wonder if she wishes this cave to be our nest.

It is rather primitive, but my ancestors once nested in caves. If they could do it, I suppose I could make do to please her. However, if she knew of my castle and the amenities my city has to offer, would she still want to nest here?

Then there is the question of mating. In my culture, there is a mating chase. Not all hold to this ritual, but many do. The male pursues the female and if he captures her, she will then either decide to accept or reject his request to become her mate. I do not know the courtship and mating rituals of Lilliana's people. She stared for a rather long time at the slit of my mating pouch; I can only hope we are compatible in that way.

Surely, we must be, else the Gods would not have blessed us with the fated bond.

Myriad thoughts tumble through my mind as I shift into my draka form. Because we are of two different species, many unknowns plague our bonding.

An image of her bare form surfaces in my mind. She is my linaya and I long to claim her in all ways. I imagine chasing her across the desert sand and capturing her in my arms. She would accept me, leaning forward on her hands and knees as I mount her from behind, filling her with my essence so that every male knows that she is mine. But I wonder if this style of mating would be too rough for my delicate mate.

First, I must prove to her that I am worthy of being hers. I will provide and care for her every need so that she knows what a capable male I am.

CHAPTER 12

LILLY

As I move to the back of the cave, I worry about Varus. He's braving the storm not because *he* needs food but because I told him that *I* did. I glance down at my arm and the *medicinal paste,* as he called it, on my wounds. He risked his life to save me from that monster.

I can't remember the last time someone took care of me. Who would go out of their way for a complete stranger?

A smile tugs at my lips. A good guy, that's who.

I think of how carefully he treated my injury. There is such kindness behind his reflective green eyes. When he studied me before he left, I started blushing like crazy.

He's handsome—for an alien, that is. Heat flushes my skin at the memory of his tall, lean, muscular build. I saw not an ounce of fat on his body; he's like a marble sculpture of pure, masculine perfection.

But I wonder about his lack of… equipment, so to speak. He was completely nude, yet I didn't see anything that even remotely resembled typical male anatomy. Maybe his species don't have what I would consider typical anatomy. I shake my head. It would be just my luck to be attracted to an alien I'm not physically compatible with.

There is something intriguing about Varus that makes me want to learn more about him and his people. The more time I spend with him, the more *human* he seems, even though he clearly isn't. He's been so kind and gentle with me. I'm becoming more comfortable with him, regardless of his dangerous appearance.

The floor is warm beneath my feet as I reach the pool. Varus said the water was safe to drink and bathe in, but as much as I want a bath, I don't want to contaminate the pool by getting in.

As I reach the edge, I notice there are actually two pools, one smaller and elevated, the other large enough to fit at least four people. We can drink from the tiny one and bathe in the larger one. Problem solved.

Raising my arm, I sniff my armpit and wrinkle my nose. Wandering around in the desert isn't exactly clean work. I could use a bath and I suppose now is as good a time as any, since I'm alone. Who knows when I'll get another chance?

Thankfully, the dimly glowing light of the gemstones embedded in the cave walls casts just enough illumination for me to see clearly. Without these, I'd probably be stumbling around in the dark.

Peeling off my clothes, I fold them neatly near the edge of the water. I always wanted to try skinny-dipping in a hot spring after reading about natural springs in some history books. By the time I was born, places like this no longer existed on Earth.

My home world started dying long before my birth. It was only a matter of time before the extinction of our race was brought on by our careless actions.

Softly shaking my head, I push my dark thoughts to the

back of my mind as I dip my toe into the water. It's warm and inviting. With Varus gone, I don't have to worry about his roaming eyes making me self-conscious. Slowly, I wade in. The pool is deep enough to submerge completely.

This is Heaven.

Leaning against the pool's edge, my thoughts return to Varus. I'm so lucky he found me when he did. I had thought the first predator that attacked me was terrifying, but the dragon that followed was so much worse. I've never been so scared in my life. Even when space pirates attacked my ship and my world fell apart while we raced to the escape pods, I was able to keep a clear head. But when that dragon loomed over me, I was so sure I was doomed. I can't imagine a worse fate than being eaten alive.

I need to get back to my people and warn them about what I've found. I mean, I suspected we'd find animal life on this world, but I had no idea there'd be dragons. I plan to ask Varus to help me find my people, though I wonder if I'm requesting too much. He's already going out of his way to feed me.

However, if we're going to survive here, life would be much easier with help from the locals.

Plus, I would love an excuse to get to know him better. Not just because I'm attracted to him; he knows the lay of the land. And if Varus's people are as friendly as he is, even better.

Lying back, I allow myself to float peacefully in the warm water, feeling the last of my tension melt away as I relax. I can't remember a time I was able to bathe like this. My entire life, I've always used a shower. Water was a precious commodity on Earth and the colony ships.

Soaking in the warm springs feels like a decadent luxury. I wonder how common these pools are in the desert. Perhaps I can convince my people to move into these caves. Our ancestors used to live like this, so it's not a huge stretch to think we could settle in this section of our new world. As a bonus, we'd be relatively safe from predators and sandstorms.

I dip my head below the water and run my fingers through the long, silken strands of my red hair, relishing the warmth and the sensation of cleanliness. If my people do decide to move into these caves, I'm definitely claiming this one for myself.

A smile tugs at my lips at the thought. We'll be alright; I can feel it. This planet may not be where we planned to land, but we *can* make a life here.

Our technology was born from a lack of precious resources. We can grow almost any crop using very little water with our soil enrichment formulas. I'm amazed that the sand here is full of nutrients, unlike the sands on Earth, which will simplify my job.

As soon as this storm passes, I'll ask Varus to escort me back to the rover and find my people. We can choose a nice plot of land nearby and begin farming as soon as possible. Our emergency rations won't last forever.

And I plan to pick Varus's brain about this planet's seasons so we can figure out what to plant first.

I wonder how far away his people live. Maybe they'd be willing to trade with us and help us search for the other escape pods.

This world may not be the ideal place for humanity to start over, but it's better than living on a ship. Things could always be worse; at least we're alive, which is more than I can say for so many. Closing my eyes, I helplessly picture Thomas' lifeless body in his sister's arms. Poor Skye. I can only imagine the grief she feels.

It took me years to regain a new sense of normal after my parents died. When I lost them to the last flu that swept through the ships, I was devastated beyond measure. For two years, I felt dead inside. I now recognize the same signs of mourning in my best friend. It's only been a week since he died, but she hides her sadness so well, most people would never know. However, I've seen her bury herself in her work, trying to organize our supplies, take inventory, and figure out what's salvageable after the crash. My best friend is hurting. I need to get back to her.

She was a communications officer and engineer on the ship, so we'll need her when we contact the rest of Varus' people. Unless we want to touch them each time we need to understand one another.

That could get old after a while.

A sudden rush of wind fills the cavern, drawing my attention in the direction of the cave's entrance. A soft scrape against stone fills the space and I freeze as I peer into the darkness ahead. The gemstones don't provide enough illumination to see the opening from here. If Varus had returned, wouldn't he announce his presence so as not to scare me?

What if another predator has found me? Or, heaven forbid, another dragon? I have nowhere to hide in these close quarters.

I remain still, listening for signs of a monster, but hear nothing over the pounding of my own pulse in my ears. Quietly, I lower my head into the water. Something large moves in the cave, so I take a deep breath and sink beneath the surface, hoping the intruder doesn't find me.

My lungs are burning and desperate for air, but I'm too scared to break the surface just yet. A shadow falls over the pool and I scream, releasing a stream of bubbles into the water—along with the last of my oxygen.

Through the wavering liquid, I look up to see a silhouette with a pair of long, twisted horns and a curtain of shoulder-length hair. Instantly, I recognize Varus staring back at me from above.

I shoot to the surface. Gasping for air, I cough and sputter as I draw in deep, gulping breaths.

Varus touches my bare shoulder. "Are you all right?"

Unable to speak, I nod.

He cocks his head to the side, regarding me. "I did not realize your species was aquatic."

"We're not."

He arches a brow while his gaze travels down my form. My cheeks heat in embarrassment when I remember that I'm completely naked. I gasp and bring my arm to my chest to cover my breasts and use my other hand to cover my mons. Quickly, I dive back beneath the water as if that will somehow hide me.

When I dive, I jerk away from his touch. A sudden splash and ripple beneath the surface rocks me to the side and I open my eyes to see Varus wading toward me. He grabs my arms and drags me out of the water. His eyes meet mine, full of unmistakable panic.

"What is wrong?" He darts a glance into the pool. "Did something grab you in there?"

"Yes!" I reply, sputtering and indignant. "A giant lizard man!"

"A *lizard—*" he stops abruptly then purses his lips. "I am not a *lizard man*. I am Drakarian."

I scramble to cover myself with my clothing.

He sighs heavily. "*That* is the problem?" He gestures to my clothes. "You were ashamed of your appearance?"

I roll my eyes. "I'm not used to being naked around strange men." Or anyone, to be honest.

He arches a brow. "I can see this will be a problem when you meet my people. Nudity is nothing to be ashamed of among my species. Many do not even bother wearing clothing."

My mouth drifts open. "You all just walk around naked all the time?"

"Many species do." His brow furrows deeply. "Is that so hard to believe?"

Sighing heavily, I shrug. "Well, okay. My people have a saying: 'When in Rome, do as the Romans do.'"

He cocks his head to the side. "I do not believe this phrase is translating correctly."

I shake my head and wave a dismissive hand at him. "Never mind. I think we'll have to change it to 'when in Drakaria,' anyway."

He gives me a puzzled look and I can't help the smile that curls my lips. He's kind of cute when he looks at me like that.

"I will give you your privacy so you may dress," he says, then turns around.

Now that his back is facing me, I take a moment to study him closely. With a tall, lean, and muscular frame, broad shoulders, and thick layers of corded muscles on his arms and legs, he's almost too perfect to be real. For an alien, that is.

His long, tapered tail twitches slightly as if agitated, reminding me that he is more than just a man. His toes and fingers are tipped with sharp, black claws, but they're not as scary as they first seemed. If anything, the dangerous, lethal edge heightens my attraction to him. And those large horns that sweep back from his head complete the package, accentuating his square jaw and aristocratic features.

When I reach out to touch his shoulder and get his attention, he turns with a devastatingly handsome smile.

Before now, I never thought I had a type, but staring at Varus, I find I've newly acquired one.

His smile is infectious, so I send one back. He takes my

hand, and I can't help but rub my thumb across his knuckles. Funny how I never noticed that his scales are smooth like silk, instead of rough like I expected when I first saw him.

He flashes another handsome grin then gently pulls me along while gesturing toward the cave's entrance. "I have brought you food," he says proudly.

Just that one word—*food*—makes my mouth begin to water. I'm so hungry I could eat almost—

My thoughts stop short when I follow his gaze. My jaw drops as my stomach twists into a violent knot. I cover my mouth with my other hand as bile rises in my throat.

I stare at the tangled mass of tan fur and black blood lying on the floor. With a sharp row of teeth and its tongue lolling out of its head, this creature is definitely dead. My gaze sweeps to Varus as a wave of nausea rolls through me.

Oh Stars, I think I'm going to throw up.

CHAPTER 13

VARUS

"I have brought you food," I state proudly, gesturing to my impressive kill. The Gods smiled upon me this day when I found this creature. It is a delicacy and I'm sure my mate will be thoroughly pleased with its taste.

Her jaw drops, then she covers her mouth. All the color drains from her face, replaced by a slightly green tinge. I lean closer, studying her curiously. "Is this a normal color variation for your people?"

"What the hell is that?" She points in disgust to her meal.

I blink several times, dumbstruck. "It is a delicacy. Hakaret are hard to find and even more difficult to kill because of their sharp teeth, but I have brought one back for you." I tip my chin up and puff out my chest, waiting for her adoration and praise.

"It's raw!" She grimaces.

"Yes," I reply, not understanding the problem. "It was recently killed. Hurry, let us eat. It is best when consumed fresh."

"You can't expect me to eat that," she says incredulously.

My chest deflates. This is not going as well as I expected. She does not seem pleased. "Why not?"

"I'll get sick, that's why. I can't eat meat unless it's cooked."

"Cooked? You mean... flamed?"

My brows shoot up to my forehead. Scorching the meat would ruin its fresh taste. No Drakarian would ever think to do this to such a glorious meal. But as my gaze travels up and down her form, I remind myself that she is an alien; her physiology and ways are different from mine.

She nods. "Yes. Do you have anything we can use to make a fire?"

Now I'm even more shocked. I hadn't expected her to be able to breathe flame like my people, but to hear that she cannot even make a simple fire is concerning. "Your race has not discovered yet how to make fire?"

Her head jerks back. "What?"

I sigh heavily. Oh, these poor humans. How did they ever manage to master space travel? Or survive at all, for that matter? Fire is a basic necessity for any civilization.

Perhaps that is why the Gods paired this one with me— they want me to keep her alive. Well, I will do so gladly. From her reaction, I assume that she is unable to properly prepare her own food, so I will help her. Who knows? Perhaps this simple act will impress her enough that she'll eagerly fall into my arms and insist upon our first mating.

Kneeling before my kill, I extend my sharp claws and proceed to skin the creature. Her eyes are wide as she watches me. I cut several chunks of meat from the bones. Recalling her flat, white teeth, I choose the softest, juiciest bits for her while setting aside the tougher pieces for myself.

When I am finished, I turn to her. "Stand back." I wait

until she is several paces away. Then I turn and breathe fire on the meat I reserved for her.

She gasps in what I hope is wonder at what a capable male I am, preparing a meal the way my mate likes.

Using my claws to spear each chunk, I cook it thoroughly. When I'm finished, I hold it out to her.

She shakes her head and I stare at her in confusion before offering her the chunk again. "This is yours," I say, realizing only now that I am not touching her, so she does not understand my words. I place a hand on her forearm.

"It's too hot," she says.

My jaw drops. First, she complained the meat was raw and now she finds it too hot?

"I apologize," I begin. "I thought you wanted it flamed."

She smiles. "I did, but it needs to cool before I eat, or else it might burn my tongue."

Ah. "Easily fixed." I nod and place her pieces on a smooth, flat stone. "This will allow it to cool."

As I work, I eye her discreetly. Her home world must have been quite the temperate, mild planet for her to be so sensitive to slight variations in temperature.

"Thanks." She smiles up at me and I notice a charming indentation in her left cheek while I allow my gaze to travel over her face. She really is the most captivating female. Her long hair is the color of flame, reminding me of the vast desert plains.

"How long have your people been stranded here?" I ask, curious to know how long they've been able to survive in the desert.

"About a week."

I regard her with newfound respect, brushing my thumb across the petal-soft skin where I grip her forearm. Although she appears delicate, her people must be heartier than I first believed if they survived without a permanent shelter for so long. The desert is as unforgiving as the vast oceans that border the Water Clan's lands. It is not easy to make a life in this place, even for my own species.

I tip my head to the side, studying her through an entirely new lens. My linaya is stronger than I realized. This is good.

As we chew our food, I notice the wounds on her forearm. Her bath has washed away the medicinal paste. Eyeing the caza root against the far wall, I gesture at her injuries. "We need to reapply your medicine."

"You mean alien spit, don't you?" She grins.

A smile quirks my lips at her teasing.

"Yes." I narrow my eyes. "Though, technically, *you* are the alien here. You realize that, do you not?"

She lifts her shoulders to her ears in that strange gesture again. "I guess you're right." She smiles again. "Let's finish eating first and then you can spit on me."

I nod. I like my female's sense of humor. "As you wish."

Carefully holding her arm with one hand, I apply the medicinal paste with the other. It does not escape my notice that she neither grimaces nor wrinkles her nose in disgust as she did earlier. Perhaps she feels more at ease around me now, more accepting of our differences. We're making progress, I think.

The storm still rages outside as the winds pick up. I'm not certain how much longer it will last, but I worry about nightfall. The air has cooled, and I notice her slight shiver as she curls into a ball, drawing her knees up to her chest and wrapping her arms around her legs with her back against the cave wall.

Fierce protectiveness fills me. I touch her forearm. "Are you cold?"

The slight chatter of her teeth answers for her, but she nods anyway.

"I can hold you, if you'd like. We can share warmth."

She stills, staring up at me with wary eyes.

I wait, knowing she is weighing whether to trust me this much. Just like a Drakarian female. None would dare allow a male to hold her unless he was her mate.

After a moment, she nods, moving closer. My hearts soar as she leans against me. Cautiously, I extend my wings from my back and wrap them around us both. At first, she freezes, but then she releases a small sigh of contentment and nestles against my side.

Happiness blooms in my chest that she allows me to hold her so intimately. We are building the beginnings of trust. Was ever a male so blessed to have his female trust him so early in their relationship?

Her sparkling green eyes meet mine. "Can we lie down?"

I nod, gently lowering us to the floor. Underneath my wings, I wrap my arms around her dainty form. I do not mind that she is smaller than a Drakarian female. If anything, her size calls forth my protective instincts. She fits perfectly against me and I revel in the sensation of her body so close to mine.

I tug her back against my chest. When she flinches slightly, I realize my mistake. She is nervous and I am acting too familiar without her permission.

She turns in my arms to face me, her gaze cautious. I give her a faint smile before closing my eyes and pretending to fall asleep, hoping that she will be able to relax and realize that I would never harm her.

I am keenly aware of her eyes upon me, but I remain as still as possible, making sure my breaths are soft and even. In truth, I wonder if I will be able to sleep this night. I've never held a female so closely before. The pull of the mate bond means my body is completely and utterly aware of everything about hers.

Her scent, the soft texture of her skin, her long, silken red hair. All of these features draw me in, threatening to overwhelm me.

I struggle to relax and pretend to sleep as she gently traces her delicate fingers up my arm and across the leathery folds of my wings.

"Beautiful," she whispers. I realize she is speaking to herself and not to me. She believes me unconscious.

I can barely keep a smile from forming on my lips at her praise. I can hardly believe I am actually holding my mate in my arms. Hearing her opinion of me evolve from "ugly lizard man" to "beautiful," makes my hearts soar. Perhaps I will not die alone after all.

Thoughts of holding her close every night fill my mind, followed by images of tracing my fingers along her delicate skin and watching her writhe beneath me as I give her pleasure. Her arms and legs wrapped solidly around my form as I enter her and fill her with my seed. My stav extends from my mating pouch at the thought.

Suddenly, I am overcome with worry. She has only just begun to trust me, and I do not wish to frighten her. Carefully, I turn just enough to angle my hips slightly away from her.

She responds by nestling even closer. Her face is tucked beneath my chin, her arm wrapped around my waist, and her leg is thrown over my hips. My hearts clench at the amount of trust she bestows in me. I thank the Gods again that this sweet female is mine. Her trust is a gift and I vow to never break it.

CHAPTER 14

LILLIANA

Awareness slowly trickles back into my mind as I awaken. Completely enveloped in warmth, I can't remember the last time I slept so well. Stretching out my arms and legs, I turn in the bed and snuggle under the covers. I rest my hand on the hard pillow beside me, feeling a steady thump beneath my palm.

My eyes snap open to find two reptilian green eyes staring back at me. My cheeks heat and my heart begins to tap a frantic rhythm as Varus' mouth curves into a devastatingly handsome smile.

"Good morning," I barely manage.

"Did you sleep well?"

Still tangled in his arms and wings, I nod. I can't believe I'm so comfortable around him. When did that happen? I only met him yesterday.

But even as this thought enters my mind, I realize why he puts me at ease. He's done nothing but try to take care of me since we met. I smile brightly at him. Varus is a good guy and

I'm lucky that he found me when he did. If he hadn't, I'd probably already be dead. It doesn't hurt that he's handsome in a masculine, rugged, alien sort of way.

Suddenly, a thought hits me. What if he's taken? My heart stops. It never even occurred to me to ask if a Mrs. Varus is waiting for him back home.

As I study him warily, I almost hate to ask, though I know I have to. I think I'm already developing feelings for him, although we just met.

"Varus?"

"Yes?"

"Do you, uh—" I lower my gaze, unable to meet his eyes as my cheeks flush with warmth. "Are you married?"

He pauses, which worries me. I lift my gaze to find him wrinkling his brow in confusion. "Married? What is that?"

"You know… do you have a wife? A mate?"

"Ah." He nods. "No, I do not have a mate."

I nearly sigh in relief, but freeze when he adds, "Yet."

"What do you mean?"

"My parents have chosen a female to be my betrothed."

My heart sinks. Of course, he's taken. He's too handsome to be single.

Worry flits across his features. "Do you have a mate?"

I shake my head. "No. I've never even had a steady boyfriend."

He tips his head to the side with a questioning look. "Boy… friend?"

"A guy to date—court, I mean."

"So, you are unmated?"

"Yes, I guess that's one way to put it."

Something flashes behind his eyes, but the emotion is gone too quickly for me to identify. His brow furrows. "What is wrong?"

"Nothing," I lie. "I just… realized there's a lot about you I don't know. I guess that's normal since we only just met."

He swallows thickly as he gives me a hesitant look. "Actually, there is something I have been meaning to share."

This piques my curiosity. "What is it?"

He opens his mouth to speak but quickly snaps his jaw shut. He lowers his gaze.

I laugh softly. "You look nervous, Varus. What is it? Come on." I playfully shove his arm. "You can tell me. I promise I can keep a secret."

Worried eyes meet mine and my heart stops. Whatever he's keeping from me, it's serious. At least he thinks so, judging by his tortured look.

"Seriously, Varus. What is it?" I press, all joking aside.

Drawing in a deep breath, he exhales slowly through his nostrils. "The monster dragon you are so afraid of," he begins.

My eyes fly toward the cave mouth as my heart hammers in my chest. "Oh my God! It's outside, isn't it? Just waiting to eat us if we try to leave?"

With a slight clench of his jaw, he shakes his head. "Actually, it is inside the cave."

I whip my head around to search as fear wraps tightly around my spine. "What? Where?"

"It is me." His voice drops so low I almost miss his confession.

"What?" I gawk at him.

"I am the monster you are so afraid of."

I roll my eyes and then playfully hit his shoulder again. "That's not funny, Varus. Is that what passes for a joke in your culture?"

"I am serious," he says with a sobering look.

The tone of his voice and his grim expression fill me with dread. I scramble away from him. To his credit, he doesn't try to stop me, instead allowing his arms and wings to fall away without resistance.

I back away until I reach the opposite wall, never taking my eyes off him as he slowly sits up then stands. My gaze rakes over his form and the truth suddenly dawns on me. Scales, wings, horns, claws, tail. How did I miss it before?

"Are you—are you saying that you can shift forms?" My voice is barely a whisper.

He nods as his tail wraps lightly around my ankle, giving me the contact I need to understand his words. "The beast you are so afraid of is my draka form."

I cover my mouth with my hand to stifle a dumbfounded gasp.

He holds up his hands in a placating gesture. "I promise I will not harm you, Lilliana. I would sooner end my life than ever cause you harm. My vow."

I'm speechless as I stare up at him. After a moment, I find my voice. "Why—why didn't you tell me sooner?"

He lowers his head. "You seemed so afraid when you spoke of the… 'dragon monster' and I… did not want you to fear me." He lifts his gaze to mine. "I vow that I would never harm you."

I've been terrible with secrets ever since my parents died. The doctor had told me she thought they were improving. In reality, my parents' condition had been deteriorating and the doctor was merely hoping for the best. She passed that misguided hope to me because she knew I would soon be an orphan. I'd like to say that I was the bigger person and eventually forgave the doctor's lies, but I never could. And now… I'll never have the chance to lay that part of my past to rest. I don't even know if she made it off the ship.

As I face Varus, memories of last night fill my mind. Completely and utterly vulnerable, I lay in his arms; he made me feel safer than I have in a long time.

"I trusted you."

The words escape my lips in a hoarse whisper, leaving my mouth before I even realize I've spoken them aloud.

His eyes are full of pain. "Forgive me," he pleads softly. "I did not intend to deceive you."

Even though I understand his reasoning, I can't overlook the hurt. My gaze shifts to the cave's entrance. The winds have died down, taking the worst of the storm with them. "Can you take me back to my people?"

An indecipherable emotion flashes across his eyes. Then he nods. "Of course." He examines my wounds. "But first, we must reapply the medicine to your arm."

As he rubs the alien spit medicine—or what he calls "medicinal paste"—he hums in the back of his throat. "It appears to be healing." His eyes flick up to meet mine. "You should eat and drink something before we leave."

Numbly, I nod.

Despite our brief time together, I was already building a connection to him. I've heard that shared survival situations can bond people very quickly. This is a whole new world for me, so maybe that's why I've grown so attached to him in such a short amount of time.

I wonder what other secrets he is keeping and decide to find out.

"So, tell me more about your people."

He tips his head to the side. "What would you like to know?"

I shrug. "Are there many of you?"

He looks at his hands. "Not as many as there once were."

His tone is full of sadness, but I cannot read his expression as he studies the floor, seeming far away.

"What do you mean?"

"A great plague swept through our population not long ago and killed many, including my older sister." He lifts his gaze to mine, his eyes bright with tears. "We were very close, she and I."

My heart clenches. I brush my fingers down his arm to take his hand, entwining our fingers. "I'm so sorry, Varus. I lost my parents a few years ago to a plague that ravaged our ships."

Gently, he squeezes my hand. "Do you have any other family?"

I shake my head and despite my attempt to rein in my sadness, an unbidden tear escapes my lashes and rolls haltingly down my cheek.

He reaches up and gently brushes the teardrop away with the soft pad of his thumb. The gesture is so sweet, it makes me cry even more. It's been so long since anyone treated me so tenderly. Closing my eyes, I allow myself to lean into his touch.

When I open them, he is regarding me with a softened expression.

"Why do I feel so comfortable with you?" I whisper, not realizing I've voiced the thought aloud until the words have already escaped my lips.

His gaze travels over my face like a gentle caress. "Because you are my fated one—my linaya. I feel the same as you."

His words puzzle me. "Fated one? What are you talking about?"

He lifts our joined hands to his chest as he stares deep into my eyes. "The moment I first saw you, I felt the pull of the fated bond. I knew then that you were mine and I was yours." He pauses. "And when this happened, I knew it to be truth."

"When what—" I start to ask but trail off as I follow his gaze to the center of his chest. His red scales begin to glow in a strange, swirling pattern beneath my palm. "What's that?"

"The fated mark only appears when a Drakarian finds his fated one—his linaya. It happened when I found you. At first, I knew by sight, but this"—he points to the glowing pattern —"proved my suspicion. However, I was uncertain whether you felt the pull, as well. Whether your species was even capable of bonding. No Drakarian has ever bonded with an off-worlder before."

I gape at him. "I don't understand. You think we're destined to be together?"

He nods, his expression resolute. "Yes." He thumps his fist to his chest. "I feel it here. You are my mate."

"But we barely even know each other," I protest.

"That will come with time," he replies matter-of-factly.

I look down, unsure of how to reply. "My people don't have a… fated bond."

He places two fingers under my chin and tips my head up. "I can see this is strange to you, so I wish to reassure you I will never ask you for anything you are not willing to give. If you need time to learn more about me before deciding to take me as your mate, I will wait until you are ready."

His words are comforting; he won't push me into anything I don't want. However, this all seems to be happening so fast.

I need to get back to my people.

As if reading my thoughts, he glances at the food he cooked for me last night. "We must find the rest of your people. But you should eat before we leave."

I'm eager to return to my friends, especially Skye, but he's right. After living on emergency rations for the past week, I'm unwilling to waste food. Especially a meal that's been cooked to my liking.

We sit across from one another and I watch him eat, my mind turning over his conviction about our fated bond. He truly believes we are destined for one another. It's a lot to take in, and I'm not sure I buy into his belief. How can we possibly know that we're right for each other? Not only are we two different species—we met less than twenty-four hours ago.

He bites into another raw chunk of meat as if it's delicious. For some reason, his eating habits don't bother me as much as they did yesterday. Despite lying to me about his nature, I still trust him not to hurt me. After all, if he wanted to, he could have done so a hundred times over by now.

When we're finished eating, he heads for the ledge, scanning the area for any sign of danger or the storm worsening. Satisfied that it's safe, he turns back to me. "Stand back while I transform into my draka form. I will prove to you that I did not lie. I may be the 'dragon' you saw, but I vow I will never hurt you."

I nod, mentally bracing myself for his scary other form.

That's another problem. I'm terrified of his dragon form. How will we overcome that?

In a whirl of dust and wind, he transforms in the blink of an eye.

The last time I saw him like this, I was on the verge of passing out due to the toxins tainting my blood. This time, I'm able to study him.

My jaw drops and I freeze in place. Varus is an enormous, towering dragon—I mean, draka—covered in deep-crimson scales. He flicks his long, tapered tail as he lowers his massive, horned head. His reflective, green-rimmed pupils contract then expand as he meets my gaze. His nostrils flare, drawing in my scent before he releases a quick huff of air that nearly knocks me over. A nervous laugh escapes me as he gently nudges my arm.

"Varus?"

He tips his head slightly to the side and arches a brow, touching the tip of his wing to my arm. "Who else would it be?" he asks, and I notice a slight upward quirk at the corners of his mouth as he teases me.

I guess this form isn't so bad now that I know it's Varus, not a strange monster.

Lowering his body, he extends his front leg. "Ready?"

I've never been particularly nimble, and my nerves make it even more difficult to scale his leg. Something wraps around my waist, startling me for a moment, before I realize his tail is carefully helping to lift me onto his back. He places me directly over his shoulders.

The long spines lining his back and tail are flattened, I notice. Probably to avoid accidentally spearing me while I'm riding him.

Once I've settled in, he turns to scan the ground below the cave.

"Uh… Varus?"

He turns his massive head toward me. "Yes?"

"You won't drop me, right?" I grin nervously.

His draka lips curl up in an approximation of a smile. "Never, my mate."

His words make my heart flutter in my chest.

CHAPTER 15

VARUS

As Lilly sits on my back, I notice something strange. She is not speaking, but in this form, I am able to sense her thoughts through the touch of her skin upon mine.

Several images flit through her mind, along with a tangled mess of emotions. I sense how nervous she is about flying, but she trusts me not to drop her.

Her faith in my ability to protect her fills me with pride.

We dip and weave through the air, following the path of the air currents. I am honored that she trusts me to carry her. Without wings, she would tumble to her death if she fell. I am glad that she is still able to trust me even though I withheld the truth of my draka form from her.

My nostrils flare and I'm instantly alert as I scent another Drakarian nearby. Drawing the scent deep into my lungs, my eyes snap open when I realize it is not a member of the Fire Clan. No, this is a Drakarian of the Wind and I recognize him almost instantly. It is my rival, Prince Raidyn of the Wind Clan.

We were as close as brothers before his mother's death. I've sparred with him in the past, but I am hesitant to meet him now. Especially with my female on my back.

Scanning the area, I search for a hiding place. When I see none, I turn and circle back, hoping he has not scented me as well.

A deafening roar splits the air a second later. Lilly's fear beats through our connection like an insistent drum, echoing my own. I do not want to fight him while she is with me. She could be harmed accidentally.

"What's that?" she yells, trying to make sure I can hear her over the wind.

"A trespasser from another Clan. I'll need to hide you."

"Why?" she responds, alarmed. "Do you think he'd try to eat me?"

If I wasn't so panicked, I'd laugh. She must think us Drakarians are a savage race indeed. Raidyn is more likely to steal her away and try to coax her to mate with him than to eat her. No matter which Clan we hail from, my kind would never eat another sentient being—especially not a female.

A towering rock formation in the far distance looks like an ideal place to conceal my mate. Furiously flapping my wings, I race toward the structure, hoping I'll make it there before Raidyn sees her.

As soon as we reach the formation, I circle just above the upper ledge and then carefully land. There is no time to wait for her to dismount by herself, so I use my tail to gently pull her off my back, setting her firmly beneath the upper ledge to shield her from his view.

I turn to find her staring up at me in concern. "Are we going to hide here?"

"You are," I tell her. "I must lead him away."

"You're going to just leave me here? Alone?" she asks incredulously. She shakes her head. "No. Stay here with me. You could get hurt out there."

Although I'm worried about her safety, I cannot help the pleasure that moves through me at her concern for my welfare. Perhaps there is hope for our relationship after all. A Drakarian female never worries about the health and safety of a male other than her mate or fledglings.

I dip my head. "I will return to you or die trying. My vow."

She huffs in frustration. "That's what I'm worried about! The dying part! Just stay here!"

A sly grin twists my mouth. She is demanding, my female, and very adamant about my well-being. This is a good sign.

Another booming roar sounds and I turn to find Raidyn racing toward us on the wind.

"Hide," I tell Lilliana over my shoulder as I untangle my tail from her waist. Extending my wings, I lift off the rocky ledge to face my rival.

Moving as fast as I can, I rush to meet him head-on. I know Raidyn; he would never hurt a female. None of our people would. But he might try to steal her away, and I cannot lose my linaya now that I've found her.

"Raidyn, stop!" I cry out, but he continues to race toward me.

We clash in a fury of teeth and claws, tumbling through the air in freefall.

"What are you doing here?" I cry as we split apart to regain some altitude. "This is Fire Clan territory! You should not be here!"

His light gray scales shimmer iridescently beneath the sun. When his ice blue eyes meet mine, my gaze travels over the long scar that runs from just above his right brow down to the top of his cheek. It is the only physical scar he bears from the day he lost his mother, but I know he carries emotional ones that run far deeper than this disfiguring injury.

He blames me and my clan for his mother's death.

His eyes burn with fire as he flares his nostrils, scenting the wind. "What are you hiding?" he growls. His gaze shoots toward the towering rock where I left Lilliana.

Fierce possessiveness burns through me like fire.

She is mine! My mate! My Lilliana! He cannot have her!

My hearts stop and then begin hammering. Instead of answering, I rush him again. Baring my fangs and claws, I tear into his thick scales.

He roars in anger, slamming into the rock with a sickening thud.

Lilly rushes from her hiding place, her gaze flicking between us with a terrified expression.

"What is that?" he growls, his nostrils flaring again. "A wingless female? She does not smell Drakarian."

"She is mine!" I grind out. "You cannot have her!"

"Yours?" He gives me an incredulous look. His eyes widen when he notices my chest. I look down to find the glowing mate pattern swirling brightly across my scales. "You have found compatible females?"

With a deafening roar, I charge him a third time, but he manages to twist away at the last moment.

"You are withholding this from our Clan? We have an alliance!" he grits through his teeth.

"I just found her. In Fire Clan territory. Why are you here? This land is not yours."

He ignores my question, growling low in his throat. "You are lying. Where did you find her?"

Indignation burns through me. "I am not lying! I was as surprised as you are to find compatible females. Especially my linaya. I found her only yesterday, wandering alone in the desert."

"Lies!" he grinds out as he swoops around me to get a better look at my mate.

I swipe at him again and he barely avoids my talons.

A feral cry of fear rips from Lilliana's throat as he twists back and attacks me. We lock onto one another, tumbling through the air and toward the ground, claws and fangs rending flesh and spilling blood as neither of us holds back.

Raidyn was once my friend. We used to be as close as brothers. But as he snaps his jaw and tears into the supporting joint of my wing, I am painfully reminded that those days are long gone.

Folding my wings against my back, I dive. His teeth tear from my wing and I roar as blinding pain rips through me.

Blood drips from our wounds onto the crimson sand below as we circle one another, spiraling through the sky in a blur of fury. His light gray scales are stained almost completely black with the blood seeping from his numerous wounds.

He slashes out at me, but I manage to dodge the blow. We are both tired and panting heavily, but I cannot allow him to take my mate. Using the last of my strength, I strike him, raking my claws across his face.

My move is almost dishonorable, given his already disfiguring scar there, but I'm desperate to repel him.

He retreats, tumbling toward the ground for a moment before his wings snap open. With several tears in the sails, he struggles to fly. His eyes are wide as they meet mine and he lifts a hand to his face, pulling it back to regard the blood that stains his scales.

My shoulders sag in relief. I didn't want to scar him any further. It is only a flesh wound, easily repaired and should leave no scarring once he reaches a Healer, but he does not know that. His eyes burn with rage as they meet mine.

"This is not over!" he yells. "I will return with more of my people!"

I open my mouth to speak but he races away, spinning around once to growl at me before heading in the direction of his kingdom.

I remember the last time I visited the verdant floating islands of the Wind Clan's territory as a child. They welcomed me as one of their own, just as Raidyn was once received in our lands. It feels like an eternity ago. My hearts are heavy like they always are when I think of those days, as I watch his form retreat into the distance.

Satisfied that he is no longer a threat, I turn back to my mate. With difficulty, I manage to land on the rocky ledge beside her. Every muscle in my body aches and throbs. Blood stains my normally crimson scales black in several places, though I know my injuries probably appear worse than I feel.

Tears flow down Lilliana's cheeks as she runs her hands over my body, assessing my numerous injuries.

"You're hurt."

Her voice quavers as she spreads her arms wide over my body, leaning against my side as if she could hug my massive form. "Tell me what to do. How do I help you? What do you need? Caza root?"

I lift my weary gaze to hers. "I need to place you on the ground, so you aren't trapped up here while I heal." I've been heavily injured before and not felt the consequences until much later. I worry that is the case now. I feel fine, but do not trust that the rush of battle isn't still running through my veins, giving me the illusion of strength. If I were to collapse or fall unconscious, Lilliana could be stuck here with no way to get down. At least on the ground, she'd have the chance to survive if I do not.

She gasps. "No! I won't leave you!"

I'm too tired to argue but another idea presents itself. I lift her into my hand, careful of my large talons, and head back to the cave we left earlier. I believe I can make it there. At least she would have water and some food to eat while I recover from my injuries.

It takes everything inside me to remain airborne all the way back to our cavern in the cliff wall. My determination to fly my mate to safety lends strength to each flap of my wings.

Luckily, the cave is only a short distance away. I will need to heal before we can travel any farther. I'm too exhausted to reach Valoria—The Fire Clan's Capital City and my home.

The cliff face in the distance is a welcome sight.

My mate gently strokes my palm. "We're almost there."

Through the touch connection, I sense her relief. Fear still lingers in the back of her mind, but she worries for my health, not her safety.

I cannot help but feel pleased with this discovery.

When we reach the cavern, my entire form shudders as I struggle to set us down on the ledge carefully. The several tears in my sails make hovering difficult, but I somehow manage.

As soon as my feet touch down, I carefully set Lilliana on the ground then transform into my two-legged form. Pain and exhaustion hit me like a giant wave. I only manage a few steps before I collapse just inside the entrance.

Lilliana wraps her arms tightly around me and pulls my head into her lap as tears stream down her face.

"Oh, Varus." Her voice quavers. "Tell me how to help you. Please, don't die on me. Tell me what to do."

I'm surprised by not only her tears but by the several soft presses of her lips to my cheek, brow, and nose. This must be how her people show concern for their mates.

My wounds are not deep enough to need caza root and I

know I'll heal naturally given enough time. She, however, does not know this. I am hesitant to inform her as she gently cups my face and strokes her hand up and down my arm in a soothing gesture. If I were to die right now, I would die happy in the arms of my linaya.

"Can you walk?" she asks softly.

I nod. Pain shoots through my body as I stand. I grit my teeth to keep from wincing with each step. When I stumble slightly, she wraps her arms around me from one side to help me walk. It is amusing that she believes she could support my weight in such a way, but I enjoy the idea of holding her, so I say nothing and simply allow her to assist me.

She leads me to the pool at the back of the cave. Releasing me, she strips until she is covered only in the small, triangular scrap of material between her thighs and the strange band of fabric wrapped around her chest.

She dips the cloth of her tunic into the water and wrings it out before gently dragging material over my scales to clean my wounds. As she works, I study her closely, appreciating the aesthetic of her form more than I did the first time I saw her in such a state of undress. Perhaps my injured state grants me this boldness as I make no attempt to avert my gaze traveling over her beautiful body.

She is mine and I long to know everything about her.

The sensuous curve of her breasts and the soft flare of her hips make my mouth go dry. My fingers flex and extend at my sides with a great need to touch her.

Already, the mating heat calls to me. I imagine parting her legs and settling between them, gripping her thighs to hold her in place as I thrust deep into her core. Her long hair falls over her shoulders in fiery waves as she kneels over me. Unable to help myself, I reach up to grasp a silken tendril, twirling it tenderly around my finger. The image of her hair spread out beneath her as she watches me with a heavy-lidded gaze while I mount her overtakes my mind.

Her lips curve into a beautiful smile and I push away my lust-filled thoughts. She has not yet given me permission to touch her in that way. Until she does, I will satisfy my desire by allowing her to lavish all her gentle concern and attention on me as she tends to my wounds.

Methodically, she works on cleansing my body from head to toe. I don't mean to fall asleep, but her hands deliver me to such a blissful state that I close my eyes and drift away to the sound of her soothing voice.

CHAPTER 16

LILLIANA

Varus closes his eyes as I tend his injuries. I listen to the sound of his breathing becoming soft and even, satisfied that he doesn't seem to be in pain.

I gently cup his face as I eye his sleeping form. "I don't want you to die, Varus. As crazy as it sounds, and I don't know if this mate bond you talked about is influencing me, but I'm starting to have feelings for you." A faint smile curves my lips. "And it doesn't matter to me that you're not human."

My gaze travels over his body and I marvel again at the perfection of his form. I trace my fingers along his toned chest and abdomen. Running my hand over the thick cords of muscle on his arm, I thread my fingers through his and gently lift his hand to my lips, pressing a soft kiss to the space between his thumb and forefinger.

He nearly died protecting me from that other Drakarian. He cares so deeply for me. Would it really be so strange to fall in love with an alien? As I study him, our differences don't seem as stark as they did when I first met him.

His build is powerful and yet he moves with a lethal, fluid grace that belies his hulking form. I study his claw-tipped fingers and a small smile curves my mouth. Though he is as deadly as he is beautiful, he's treated me so tenderly in the time we've been together.

Ever since my parents died, I've been fiercely independent. I've had to be. I have no one to rely on but myself. Sure, I have friends, but that's different. Varus hardly even knows me, but he cares for me better than anyone. Would it be so bad to fall for a man who wants only to provide for me? To love me?

I lean down and place a sweet kiss to his cheek, whispering against his skin. "Thank you for protecting me, Varus."

After I finish cleaning his injuries, I chew some of the caza root into a fine paste and hope that it doesn't make me sick. It's a risk worth taking since it would be impossible for me to survive without him. The taste is disgusting, but it's the least I can do since he was injured protecting me. Besides, I want to take care of him the way he took care of me when we first met.

Carefully, I rub the medicinal paste into his wounds. I'm astonished to find the torn tissue already beginning to knit together.

I glance down at my injured forearm. While it's healing, my recovery rate is nowhere near his. This root must work much better on his people, which I suppose is to be expected. After all, Drakarians evolved on this planet and my race did not.

Satisfied that he is beginning to heal, I carefully lie down beside him. I rest my head on his shoulder and my arm across his chest, placing my open palm directly over the swirling pattern of glowing scales. I'm surprised to feel two heartbeats instead of one. I enjoy the comforting sensation of the steady beat beneath my hand, reminding me that he's alive and safe beside me.

I allow my gaze to travel over his face. A faint smile curls my lips as I whisper sweetly, "I think I'm falling in love with you."

With his eyes still closed, he lifts his hand and rests it gently atop mine over his chest. I smile again as the faint glowing pattern swirls beneath my palm before they disappear again. I nestle closer to him and close my eyes as I drift into oblivion.

Awareness slowly trickles back into my mind and I lift my head to find Varus already awake and watching me. His reflective green eyes hold mine as a devastatingly handsome smile curves his mouth.

He reaches across and gently brushes the hair back from my face, tucking a stray tendril behind my ear. "The words you spoke last night," he whispers. "Did you mean them?"

I tip my head to one side. "What words?"

"You said you are falling in love with me."

My mouth drifts open as my cheeks heat in embarrassment. "You heard that? I thought you were asleep."

"Please." He takes my hand in his. "Tell me, Lilliana. Are you falling in love with me?"

My heart melts at his vulnerable expression and I nod, suddenly self-conscious beneath his expectant attention. As if his every wish and dream hang on this moment, on my answer. "I... know it's sudden since we only just met, but... yes, I think I'm falling in love with you."

He places two fingers under my chin and tilts my head up to meet his eyes evenly. "You are the most beautiful female I have ever seen."

My breath hitches in my throat as he regards me like I'm a rare and precious thing, his gaze traveling over my face like a gentle caress. Something about his expression draws me closer and I lean in, closing the space between us until my face is less than an inch from his.

His warm breath fans across my skin. He smells like cinnamon and some exotic spice—a heady scent that I can't quite place but is so familiar somehow. His gaze holds mine as I gently press my lips to his.

His lips are warm and softer than I imagined. He inhales sharply when I pull back, staring at me in wonder.

"Do your people not kiss, Varus?"

He reaches up and lightly touches his mouth. "Kiss," he whispers, more to himself than to me. "Is that what this is? This pressing of lips?"

A short puff of air escapes me and I smile, amused at his description. "Yes."

"What does it mean?"

My entire face flushes with warmth as I lower my gaze from his, nervous that he may not like this. That perhaps I've been too forward and done something he doesn't want.

"It means," I begin shyly, "that I like you. That I'm... interested in you."

"As a mate?"

"Yes."

He's quiet for so long I wonder what he's thinking. Suddenly, he leans in and presses his lips to mine in a tender kiss. He wraps his arms around me, pulling me even closer.

I trace my tongue along the seam of his lips, asking for entrance. He gasps and my tongue finds his, curling around it and deepening our kiss.

His mouth is warm and tastes of spice and cinnamon. The ridged texture of his tongue as it moves against mine only adds to the delicious sensations moving through me.

At first, he's slow and almost hesitant, allowing me to lead, but eventually, he takes control. His tongue moves against mine passionately, stealing the breath from my lungs and filling me with a desire unlike any I've ever felt before.

I've kissed a few guys on dates, but those were never like this. This is a powerful, raw, and all-consuming passion. His hands are everywhere, all at once, as if he cannot get enough of touching me.

He rolls me beneath him, and I wrap my arms around his neck, running my fingers through the small hairs at the nape. I trail my hands down his back, kneading the muscles along the length of his spine. His scales are soft and smooth as silk beneath my touch.

I only meant to kiss him, but as his hips settle between my thighs, I'm desperate for more. My entire body feels as if it's on fire and I want him to touch me everywhere.

Taking his hand, I move it down my body to my breast. "Touch me here," I whisper against his lips.

A low growl rumbles in his chest and he rips his mouth from mine, trailing kisses along my jaw and down my neck to the valley between my breasts. He gently squeezes the soft mound, brushing his thumb across the already stiff peak. A soft moan escapes me, and I arch into his palm.

"May I kiss you here?" he whispers, staring up at me with a heavy-lidded gaze.

"Please," I beg.

He lowers his head to run his tongue along the slope of my other breast. When he closes his mouth over the peak and swipes his tongue across the beaded tip, I gasp then moan, running my fingers through his hair and holding him close against me. "Feels so good, Varus."

Encouraged by my reaction, he continues to lave at my left breast before moving to the other and giving it the same attention.

I've heard others talk about sex, but I've never even fooled around with anyone. All of this is new to me and I can't get enough. I finally understand what all the fuss is about as I wrap my arms and legs around him to hold him close.

It doesn't matter that he's an alien and different from me. He's Varus and I want him more than I've wanted anyone in my entire life.

He trails kisses further down my body until he reaches my mons. Lifting his head, his eyes meet mine full of unmistakable hunger. "May I touch you here?"

Unable to speak, I nod.

He lowers his head and his tongue swipes through my folds and over the small bundle of nerves at the apex. I gasp and arch against him, desperate for more.

He growls low in arousal as he runs his hands over my thighs, opening me further to his gaze. "You are perfect," he says, his voice full of reverence.

Carefully, he pulls my legs over his shoulders then returns his attention to the sensitive bud, tracing his tongue over the hooded flesh until I'm gasping and panting beneath him.

He bands one arm across my hips to hold me in place as he continues to explore my body. I gasp again when he gently inserts one finger into the entrance of my core. Slowly, he thrusts in and out until he reaches a sensitive spot that sends me soaring to new heights of pleasure.

The small muscles of my channel flex and quiver around his finger until I'm desperate.

"Varus." His name escapes my lips in a breathless whisper. "I want you."

"I am here," he answers. "I am here, my linaya."

He concentrates his attention on my folds once again, swiping his tongue across the sensitive pearl at the apex. I moan as his finger moves in and out of my core, creating the most delicious friction.

I'm so close, I'm nearly there.

He growls, low in arousal, and the sound vibrates through my core, heightening my desire. My entire body goes taut for a moment before I cry out his name as wave after wave of pleasure washes through me. He continues to lap at my folds, wringing out every last second of my orgasm, until I gently push him away. I tug at his shoulders and he moves back up my body until his face is even with mine.

I cup the back of his neck and pull his lips down to me, capturing his mouth in a passionate kiss. Something hard and warm bumps against the entrance to my core and I gasp at the sensation.

He pulls back and I glance down my body to see the hard length of his erection. It seems he does have similar anatomy to human males. I reach down and wrap my hand around his length. He's so large, my fingers can't reach all the way around him.

The breath explodes from his lungs as I gently stroke his length. "My stav is very sensitive," he rasps.

I explore him. His stav is like soft silk over hard steel. His entire length is covered with layers of ridges and I try to imagine how that will feel inside me.

I position his tip at the entrance to my channel and wrap my legs around his hips in encouragement. "I want you, Varus."

He stares down at me in wonder. "You would already accept me into your body?"

Shyly biting my lower lip, I nod. "Yes."

He kisses me again but then gently pulls back. "I am honored that you choose me to be yours, Lilliana, but we cannot mate yet."

I wrinkle my brow. "Why not?"

Gently, he brushes the hair back from my face as he regards me, his gaze fiery and possessive. With a slight clench of his jaw, he sighs heavily.

"I am feeling better, but I am not fully recovered yet from my battle with the Wind Drakarian." He skims the tip of his nose along mine and growls low, sounding frustrated. "And I want our first mating to last several hours."

My toes practically curl at the thought as he captures my mouth in a claiming kiss.

He pulls back and his nostrils flare as his eyes meet mine, his lids heavy with desire. "I can scent your need, my mate. I long to enter your body and fill you with my seed so that every unmated male within several arcums will know you are mine and mine alone."

Something about his caveman-like declaration makes my heart flutter.

"Tell me you are mine," he growls, his eyes ablaze. "I need to hear it."

A small part of my mind tells me this is happening too fast, but another, more insistent part reminds me that I could have died several times over since our ship was attacked by pirates. Life is short and fleeting. So, if this gorgeous man wants me, I am all in. This is a new world, a new life, and I plan to enjoy as much of it as I can.

I reach up and cup his cheek. "I'm yours," I agree. "And you're mine."

He flashes his handsome smile and pulls me into his arms, hugging me close. "I never imagined that I would be so blessed with such a perfect mate," he whispers into my hair.

Tears sting my eyes and emotions lodge in my throat as I pull away to gaze up at him. I cup the back of his neck and tug his lips down to mine, showing him how much his words mean to me.

To pass the time while Varus recovers, we explore each other. I tell him about my life on the ship, my friends, and how we've survived since we crashed on this planet. How every day, we hold out hope that more survivors are out there somewhere.

As we talk, he tenderly brushes the tips of his fingers up and down my arm and then over my bare shoulder and back as if memorizing my body through touch, and I do the same.

"You said the other draka was a Wind Drakarian. What does that make you?" I ask, curious about his world.

"There are four Clans: Fire, Wind, Water, and Earth. My people are of the Fire Clan."

"And the rest are your enemies?"

He shakes his head softly. "No. We have an uneasy alliance with each, but of the other three, the only Clan I truly trust is the Earth Clan. Most of them work as Healers among our people, so they have always been neutral."

"Did you know the draka who attacked you?"

He nods. "He is Raidyn. Prince of the Wind Clan and my rival for you."

"For me?"

"Females are scarce," he explains. "After the great plague that swept through the Clans, many of our females died, including my older sister, Laris. Of those that are left... many are sterile."

His expression grows sad as he mentions his sister. I reach out to cup his cheek. "I'm sorry about your sister, Varus."

"It has been three cycles, but I still miss her," he murmurs.

"My parents died three years ago, too. It was so hard watching them suffer before they passed. I think about them every single day. I think it's normal to miss the ones you've lost so much."

He hugs me close, tucking my head under his chin as he nods in a tiny movement. "I believe my sister would not have liked you."

Taken aback by his comment, I pull away just enough to fix him with a mildly offended look. "Why? Because I'm... different?"

A sly grin twists his lips. "She was very protective of me and always teased that no female would be good enough for her younger brother."

I laugh. "Well, if she'd ever had a chance to meet me, she would have changed her mind, because *I* am wonderful."

"No," he answers seriously. He reaches out to gently cup my face, tracing the soft pad of his thumb across my cheek. "You are perfect, my linaya."

A smile curves my lips a moment before he captures my mouth in a passionate kiss, leaving me breathless and wanting.

When he finally pulls back, he whispers tenderly, "Rest, my mate. I should be well enough that we can leave this cave in the morning."

Curling up in his arms, I rest my head on his chest and close my eyes as he wraps his wings tightly around us.

I could get used to sleeping like this every night.

CHAPTER 17

VARUS

Whcn I wake in the morning, I notice that almost every ache and pain of the last day has vanished. I am not entirely healed yet, but I am ready to leave this place. I am eager to take Lilliana to my people, introduce her to my parents, and proudly announce to our subjects that she is mine.

I lean down and gently nuzzle her hair, inhaling her delicate scent deep into my lungs.

She stirs lightly in my arms then lifts her head to look at me. "Good morning." She gives me a sleepy smile. "How are you feeling?"

"Fully recovered," I reply. "Now that you are awake, we can fly to meet my people."

"Your people? I thought you were taking me to mine?"

"Now that Raidyn has seen you, he will hunt for your kind."

"What? Why?"

"As I mentioned before, there are few females left in our race. All are now considered precious."

Her brow furrows deeply as if my answer troubles her. A question lingers just behind her eyes. I wait patiently for her to ask, but she remains silent.

I continue instead. "We need to return to my city so that my warriors can accompany us to retrieve your friends. We can bring them back to our city and protect them."

Worried green eyes meet mine as she reaches up to gently trace the pronounced line of my brow. "Are you sure you feel well enough to fly?"

"Yes." I pause and wonder if her question held a hidden meaning. Is she as eager as I am for our first mating? "I suggest you eat and drink before we leave. It will not be safe to stop for sustenance in case the Wind Clan is searching for us."

"How far is your city?"

"Valoria is less than half a day's travel. But before we leave, I must check on your injury."

She smiles. "It's fine, Varus. Look." She raises her forearm proudly. "It's already healing."

Deep, red gashes mar her forearm. Although they are no longer bleeding, they are far from healed. I suspect, however, that her species does not heal as quickly as mine, because she seems pleased with the minimal progress her wound has made.

This presents yet another problem. My concerns for her safety have grown exponentially. I can only hope that our fledglings, if we can have any, inherit my natural healing abilities and defenses. I will be a stressed male indeed if our fledglings are all born defenseless like my beautiful mate.

"I would like for the Healer to assess your wounds once we reach the castle."

Her brows shoot up to her forehead. "Castle?"

I nod.

"You live in a castle?" she asks incredulously.

"Yes. Contrary to what you may believe, my people are not primitive." I arch a brow at her. "We do not live in caves."

She laughs. "Still upset about that, huh?"

"My race is very advanced," I protest. "Just because we choose to isolate ourselves from most other space-faring races does not mean that ours is a primitive existence."

She frowns. "How many other 'space-faring races' are out there?"

"Thousands."

Her jaw drops. "But this planet is relatively safe, right? From pirates and such?"

I can only imagine how devastating the space pirate attack on her ships must have been to instill such fear in her. I move quickly to assuage her worries. "You need not worry. We possess excellent defense technology."

She releases a sigh and relaxes in my arms. "That's good to hear."

I tip my head to the side. "Do you know what species attacked your ships?"

She shakes her head. "They looked a bit like your people, but more lizard-like. They had green scales and the same vertically slit pupils, but no wings. And somehow, they were able to speak our language."

The word *lizard* does not translate for me, but her description of their eyes and advanced communication tech tells me the pirates must have been Rovarans, a disgusting race. They are known throughout the quadrant as mercenaries of the lowest kind, many of them slavers.

"I believe you encountered Rovarans. They are easily dealt with. You do not need to fear them anymore. My people will keep yours safe."

She leans against me. "Thank goodness," she says, shivering slightly. "They were terrifying."

I rub her shoulders in a soothing gesture. "I will kill any who dare try to harm you. My vow."

She smiles up at me and I marvel again at her beauty. With hair the color of flame, almost perfectly matching my scales, our fledglings will be quite handsome, I believe.

"Will your people help us search for other survivors?"

I nod. My race will not hesitate to do this, especially once they find out one of their females has become my linaya. If the Gods saw fit to bind us together, I wonder how many others of our race could be meant for hers.

I suppose we will soon find out.

I glance toward the cave entrance. "You should eat, so we may leave."

I'm surprised by how quickly she consumes her meal. She is anxious to leave this place, I suspect, for fear of Prince Raidyn or his Wind Clan finding us. I share her concern. I would not be so worried about Raidyn alone, but by now, he has probably reported his discovery back to his Clan. I wouldn't be surprised if dozens of Drakarians search the desert for us even now. The idea of finding a female would be tempting enough to cross into our territory in force, further violating our treaty.

When Lilliana has finished eating, I move to the mouth of the cave. I hesitate a moment before I transform. My injuries are still healing, so the shift will most likely be painful. But I do not want to waste time. I fear that if we wait until I am completely healed to leave, we might be too late to locate her people before the Wind Clan does.

I turn back to my mate, touching her with my tail. While I

will be glad when Healer Ranas installs a translator in her ear, I will miss the constant opportunity to touch my linaya to communicate with her. I shall endeavor to find excuses to continue touching her. My need to feel her soft skin beneath my fingers is too great to be ignored.

"Step back," I warn. "I do not wish to harm you."

She moves away and I close my eyes, beginning to shift. Pain ripples through me as I change, but it dissipates quickly. Extending my wings, I test their strength. I'm surprised that I feel only a little sore. I should have no trouble reaching my city now.

I turn to my mate and gently lower my body to the ground. I reach for her with my tail, but she grins and playfully bats me away, insisting she can climb up herself.

Her surefooted ascent takes me by surprise. Perhaps she is no longer afraid of my draka form.

Once she settles between my shoulders, I stretch my wings and dive off the side of the cliff, catching the air current in my sails and lifting into the sky.

Through the touch of her skin upon mine in this form, I am once again able to overhear her thoughts. Experiencing the inner workings of her mind is strange. Her consciousness brims with a tangle of emotions: exhilaration, anxiety, joy, wonder.

As we cross the desert plains, she marvels at the landscape below. The wind is strong, sweeping a fine blanket of dust and mica across the dunes and around the towering rock formations. Footprints dot the crimson sand up ahead and she surmises correctly that they must belong to one of the many predators that hunt in this desolate landscape.

The high plateau ahead marks the outer edge of Valoria. As I ascend to pass over the steep wall, she panics, holding my spikes tightly, afraid she will fall.

"I will not drop you," I call over my shoulder, loud enough

for her to hear. I am pleased when she relaxes slightly, happy to find that she trusts my words. This is good. Trust is important between mated pairs.

When we reach the top of the plateau, I quickly cross the expanse and swoop down on the opposite side toward the wide river below. She marvels at the lush, green farmlands along the river, comparing it to images of her home world before it was poisoned by her ancestors. The mesa on the other side of the water draws her attention. She gapes in awe at the castle above—my home.

Red-orange towers spiral toward the sky as if reaching for the small wisps of clouds overhead, built as much for aesthetics as for defense. She is impressed by the beautiful gold domes atop the towers that mark the four corners of the massive structure, along with a fifth, larger tower in the middle.

As I experience my home through her eyes, I realize how little I've appreciated its beauty. To me, the castle is a common sight, one that I've seen every day of my existence.

I am pleased that she enjoys the view, however. Especially since this will be the new home of her people.

When we reach the castle, I notice several of the guards eyeing me from their posts. I expect that my parents have been frantic with worry since I left. I am their only remaining child, and I missed the betrothal ceremony they spent months negotiating with the Water Clan.

Dread fills me at the thought of facing my father. He will be so disappointed when I refuse to take Noralla as my mate. But hopefully, he will understand once I introduce my true linaya.

I also pray the Water Clan does not take offense at my rejection of their princess. While I am certain Noralla will not be particularly upset, I do not want to be responsible for damaging the already fragile peace between our two Clans.

When I touch down carefully on the balcony of my bedroom, I hear the alarm in Lilliana's thoughts.

"What are we doing here?" she asks in wide-eyed wonder as she peers through the window at my expansive chambers.

The word palatial flits through her mind, along with impressions of luxurious decadence and comfort.

A smile curls my lips. All of this wealth and comfort is now hers to enjoy.

I shift into my two-legged form and open my mouth to reply when my mother rushes through the door. "Where have you been?"

Instead of answering, I instinctively spread my wings wide to shield Lilliana as fierce protectiveness fills me.

My mother is instantly curious. "What are you doing? Where have you been? Do you know how worried your father and I were while you were gone?"

She fires off a series of questions so fast I am unable to form an answer to any.

Lilliana's small hand alights on my back, drawing my attention, and I lower my wings as she moves to stand beside me.

"What is this?" Mother's eyes widen in alarm. "Who is this?"

I cannot help the smile that quirks my lips. "This is my fated mate, my linaya, Lilliana."

I don't miss the puzzled look on Lilliana's face as she studies my mother. Suddenly, I remember that she cannot understand anyone but me. I can hardly wait for the Healer to fit her with a translator chip.

"I found her wandering in the desert and saved her. Twice." I look over Mother's shoulder into the hallway. "Where is Father?"

"Linaya?" my mother demands in disbelief as she gestures animatedly toward Lilly. "But she is not Drakarian."

"It does not matter," I reply. "She is my fated one. I feel it here." I thump my fist to my chest and watch as the glowing fate bond pattern swirls brightly between my two hearts. "The Gods have blessed us. Of this I am certain."

She blinks several times in shock before shifting her gaze to Lilly. "That creature cannot be your mate, my son."

"But—"

Lilliana squeezes my arm to get my attention. "That's your mother?"

I nod.

She turns to Mother and gives her a nervous smile, waving shyly. Mother continues to ogle her, stunned.

"Varus?" Lilly asks.

"Yes?"

"She looks kind of upset. What's she saying?"

"She is happy to meet you." The lie escapes my tongue before I can change my mind. I grin nervously.

Lilliana smiles, full of hope. "She is? She doesn't think I look strange?"

I turn and take both of her hands in mine. "You are beautiful, my mate. Why would you ever think such a thing?"

Mother clears her throat and I spin back to face her. She crosses her arms over her chest, darting a glance at Lilliana. "She doesn't have any idea what I'm saying, does she?"

I rub the back of my neck and hesitate for a moment before I reply. "Her species does not have translator chips."

Mother's jaw drops. "What kind of primitive species do not possess translating tech?"

A low growl escapes me.

"Don't you growl at me," Mother snaps. "Are her people even part of the Galactic Federation of Planets?"

"No," I admit hesitantly. Before she can interject, I ask, "Where is Father? We need to find the rest of my mate's people before the Wind Clan does."

My mother approaches Lilliana and then gasps. "Please tell me there are scales beneath her clothing."

I run a hand roughly through my hair. "Humans do not have scales. Or claws. Or fangs. Or wings," I add, figuring I might as well give my mother all the stunning news at once.

"She's defenseless?" My mother's face is aghast. "How will she protect her fledglings?" Her eyes go wide as they meet mine. "Can she even have fledglings with you?"

I huff a heavy sigh of frustration as my mother wrings her hands, mumbling to herself about being robbed of any chance for grandchildren.

Lilliana tugs on my hand. "She looks even more upset now, Varus. What is she saying? She doesn't like me, does she?"

My mate is as smart as she is beautiful, and I realize I cannot lie to her—not even to shield her from harsh judgment. "She's worried that your species doesn't have any natural defenses like ours does."

Mother crosses her arms over her chest and sends me a pointed look. "If I were you, I would not be so eager to see your father. After you left, he was forced to explain to the Water Clan that you had disappeared, and we did not know where to find you. They, of course, took offense on behalf of Princess Noralla. Fortunately for you, she agreed to remain here until your return. It seems at least one of you is interested in maintaining the peace between our Clans."

I clench my fists, resigned. She's right. If my mother is having a hard time accepting Lilly, I can only imagine how Father will react.

But I cannot change the will of the Gods, nor do I wish to. My mate is perfect. The sooner we retrieve her people, the sooner we can begin our new life together.

I turn to her. "I think we should consult the Healer. He

125

can check your wounds," I gesture to her forearm, "and fit you with a translator chip."

To my mother, I say, "I will speak with Father when we return."

With Lilliana's hand in mine, I brush past my mother to head for the Healer. We're almost out the door when my father appears on the threshold.

"No," he demands, "you will speak to me now."

I meet his icy glare. When his gaze lands on Lilliana and our joined hands, his jaw drops.

"What is this?" He points accusingly. "Who is this creature and why are you holding her hand?"

Indignation burns through me and I pull Lilly behind me, shielding her from my father's anger. "You will show her respect," I growl. "She is my linaya."

He blinks several times. "How is this possible? She is not Drakarian. She cannot be your fated one. No one has ever found a fated mate outside of our race."

I tilt my chin up to meet his eyes evenly. "Then *we* are the first."

Lilly peeks out from behind me. "Is that your dad?"

I nod.

Father's expression grows thunderous. "How can you do this? Do you realize what your little rebellion could do to our alliance with the Water Clan? This could mean war between our people."

He starts toward me and my muscles ripple beneath my scales as I struggle to keep my anger from pushing me into my draka form. Clenching my jaw, I draw in a deep breath, attempting to steady my emotions. I cannot shift now. In this small, enclosed space, I might injure my mate.

Lilliana scoots closer to my side. "He really looks like he doesn't like me. At all, Varus."

I send her another nervous smile. "He's angry with me for disappearing for two days."

She purses her lips, not believing my lie as she gestures to my mother. "And what about her? Are you going to tell me that's her *I'm-happy-to-meet-you* face?"

I lower my head, unable to hold her gaze and unwilling to lie anymore. "Forgive me," I whisper. "I just do not want to upset you."

My hearts clench at her faint smile. "It's all right, Varus. I'm sure I'm"—she looks down, gesturing at her form —"something of a shock to them."

I bring her hand to my lips and place a soft kiss to the space between her thumb and forefinger before I turn to glare at my father. "Calm down. You are scaring my mate."

"He looks even more upset than your mother," Lilly adds.

Unfortunately, my mate is perceptive. I turn and gently tuck a stray tendril of hair behind her ear as I stare deep into her luminous green eyes. "I am sorry, my linaya. You are the first fated mate of a different species. My parents are..." I cast about for a word that will not offend her. Drawing a blank, I finally finish, "stunned that you are my fated one. They will need some time to understand."

She turns to face them, her eyes bright with tears as she places one hand over her hearts. "I don't want to come between you and your son. I love him, but I... I lost my parents three years ago, so I understand how important family is."

My father's expression softens as my mother blinks back tears of her own.

When they don't speak, Lilly turns to me. "They can understand me, right?"

I nod, then address them. "Lilliana is my fated one and I will not take anyone else as my mate." She rewards me with a brilliant smile and happiness blooms in my chest, cementing my resolve. "Mother. Father. You cannot change the will of the Gods who sent her to me."

I gesture at the spot on my chest directly over my beating hearts. "Here. If you need proof, here is the fated mark upon my scales."

My father gapes as the pattern swirls across my chest. "It is truth," he whispers to himself.

"And there are more of her people. Females," I add. "They are lost in the desert and need our help to survive. While Lilliana and I were searching for them, we came across Raidyn. He saw my mate and—"

My father interrupts. "There are more females?"

"Yes."

He turns to my mother. "The Gods would not have paired them if this species' females were not biologically compatible with our race." He pauses. "Do you realize what this could mean?"

Understanding dawns on my mother's face and she smiles. "We still have a chance at grandchildren."

I struggle to bite back a sigh of frustration. Grandchildren are all my mother seems to care about these days. The moment Noralla arrived, Mother decided to start decorating the room adjoining mine as a nursery for our future fledglings.

I continue. "Raidyn and I fought, but I managed to defeat him. However, I'm certain the Wind Clan is searching for Lilliana's people already. We must find them first and bring them to our city, where we can protect them."

My father curls his fists at his side in anger. "In attacking you, Raidyn has broken the alliance. We cannot allow his Clan to capture the females, nor can we allow his transgression to go unpunished."

I lower my gaze, not bothering to tell him that Raidyn and I have sparred several times before. He is the one I seek out when I am angry and in need of a fight. We used to spar in tests of strength as children, releasing our aggression on each other. I'd like to think some sliver of our friendship still survives even though he blames our people for the death of his mother. After all, I have no wish to start a war with his Clan.

"I agree. But instead of declaring war upon the Wind Clan, we should simply concentrate on finding my mate's people."

Father gives me a solemn nod. "I will gather our best warriors to escort you into the desert and retrieve her people."

I nod. "While you do, I will take Lilliana to the Healer to tend her wound."

"Wound?" my mother repeats with wide eyes, suddenly concerned about the mate she dismissed so easily earlier. "What happened? Did Raidyn—"

I shake my head emphatically. Raidyn may have lost his way, but he is Drakarian first and foremost. A Drakarian would never injure a female. "No. She was attacked by a sand tarkin."

"What are you waiting for?" Mother demands. "Take her to the Healer immediately and get her a translator chip while you're there."

I turn to Lilliana with a grin. "See? Now they like you."

She smiles at both my parents as we leave my chambers.

When we cross the threshold, my father calls after us.

"I'll assemble the warriors. We leave at first light."

CHAPTER 18

VARUS

As we make our way to the Medical Center, it's hard to ignore the gawking people as we pass. Many of them whisper under their breath about my mate's strange appearance. I'm glad that she does not have a translator chip yet, or the stares might make her self-conscious.

Lilliana tugs on my arm. "What are they saying? Are they talking about me?"

I don't want to tell her, but I'm reluctant to lie again, so with a heavy sigh, I admit the truth. "Yes. They find your appearance… unique."

To my surprise, she lifts her shoulders with a warm smile. "I guess I'm the alien here, aren't I?"

A teasing smirk twists my lips. "And a strange one, at that."

Her jaw drops in mock offense, but then she laughs and playfully hits my arm with a bright smile. "Well, you seem to like my appearance just fine. That's all that matters."

I cannot help the joyous smile that crests my lips. She

cares not what others think of her—including other males, which means she is interested only in me. I wrap my arm around her waist and tug her closer.

She is mine and I cannot wait to fully claim her.

We continue toward the Healer in silence. I notice one of the servants walking past and call to her. "Excuse me."

She stops in her tracks, turning to face me with a deep bow before straightening. "Yes, Prince Varus?"

"This is my mate, Lilliana. Send some refreshments to my rooms for her to enjoy later."

"Yes, my prince." She bows again.

"Could you please make sure the meat is cut into tiny pieces?" I add, remembering my mate's flat, blunt teeth.

Her brow furrows slightly before she bows a third time. "Of course, my prince."

"Thank you," I smile and continue down the hall.

As soon as we arrive at the Medical Center, the Healer emerges to greet us. Ranas hails from the Earth Clan and I consider him a good friend. His smile tips into a frown of confusion as his gaze falls on Lilliana. "Who is—"

I cut him off abruptly, grinning. "This is my fated one, Lilliana. She is human and comes from the planet Earth."

"Human." He repeats the word with a contemplative expression. "I have never heard of this species or planet." He bows to her, bending deep. "Are you part of—"

"She needs a translator chip," I inform him at my mate's confused face.

He frowns again. "So, her species is not part of the Galactic Federation of Planets?"

I sigh heavily. "No, they are not." Ignoring his surprise, I turn to my mate. "This is Ranas. He is a Healer. He will assess your wound and fit you with a translator chip."

She shoots him a curious glance before turning back to me. "He's green. The rest of your people are different shades of red or orange, from what I've seen. And Raidyn was light gray. Does each Clan have scale colors particular to them?"

I mentally chastise myself for forgetting to explain Drakarian coloring. I forget this world is entirely new to her. Her people never heard of mine before now.

"Ranas is of the Earth Clan. Their Clan is neutral and thus on friendly terms with all others. Many of their people are Healers. His people tend to have scales in varying colors of greens and browns."

"Oh," she says. "Can you ask him to give me the translator chip first? I'd like to be able to understand your people."

I nod and turn expectantly to Ranas. He motions for us to follow him into an exam room.

Lilliana sits on the exam table and I give her hand a reassuring squeeze. "It will hurt a bit, but the pain should pass quickly."

All the color drains from her face. "It's painful?"

"Only for a moment," Ranas chimes in.

I translate. "He says it will not last long."

She eyes him warily as he approaches, subconsciously moving closer to me. My protective instincts soar, and I want to roar my happiness to the stars that she seeks comfort from me like a Drakarian female who has already accepted her mate.

Ranas carefully places the injector behind her left ear. She gasps at the sharp *click* that sounds when the translator embeds beneath her skin. Squeezing her eyes shut, she curls into me, struggling against the pain while gripping my arm tightly.

My hearts clench and I wrap my wings protectively around her to provide comfort. I cannot stand to see her suffering. An unbidden growl rises in my chest as I face Ranas.

"I thought it was only supposed to last a moment," I accuse through gritted teeth.

He looks baffled. "It is. I—I do not understand why—"

He breaks off when she lifts her gaze to mine, wiping away her tears. "Don't blame your friend. The pain is fading," she murmurs, giving me her best reassuring grin.

Another tear slips down her cheek and I level a dark gaze at Ranas. "You hurt my mate," I grind out. "Use your healing fire to soothe her pain. Now."

"Healing fire?" She blinks.

"Earth Drakarians can heal wounds and injuries with their healing fire," I explain. "Do not worry, it does not burn. The wound will feel better in a moment."

Her mouth drifts open slightly at my words. Ranas moves toward her and leans down, gently blowing a stream of blue-green flames behind her ear.

At first, she tenses, but the minute the soothing effect begins to take hold, her entire body relaxes against me, her pain forgotten. A light moan escapes her and my possessive instincts flare to life. This sound is suspiciously similar to the mewls of pleasure she made in the cave. I glare at my friend and he subtly backs away.

She smiles up at me. "Wow! It worked. My ear doesn't hurt anymore."

While I am pleased she is no longer in pain, I send Ranas another warning glare. The message is clear: *She is my mate, not yours.*

He dips his chin in an imperceptible bow and takes another step back. From his supply table, he pulls out a scanner. He looks to me and I realize he is waiting for permission to scan my mate.

I turn to Lilliana. "He is going to scan you now, to assess your wounds. Is that all right with you?"

She nods and he takes a cautious step toward her, close

enough to run the scanner over her form while still keeping a respectful distance from my mate. Part of me is ashamed to act so hostile toward my friend, but another realizes that my behavior is natural for a newly mated male. Until we complete the bond and I have fully claimed her, my instincts will demand that I chase other males away.

With a heavy sigh, I regard my friend. "I apologize for my behavior."

He gives me a friendly smile. "All is well. You are acting on instinct, Varus. Nothing more."

Ranas is an honorable male.

The scanner beeps a few times as he examines her wound. "It appears to be mending nicely." he tips his head to the side. "Strange, however, that your species heals so slowly. My readings indicate this is a normal progression of recovery for your injury."

As he scans the remainder of her body, the scanner beeps again. His brows furrow deeply as he studies the readout.

Anxious, she asks, "What is it? Is something wrong?"

Her concern echoes my own as I hold my breath, waiting for an answer.

Ranas lifts his gaze, blinking several times. "You and the prince can have fledglings together."

"What?" she asks, obviously surprised. "But we're completely different species."

He nods. "Yes, but your species' biology appears to be adaptive. You most likely would require some sort of medical intervention, but it should be possible for you to conceive with the prince and carry his fledglings."

I want to roar my joy to the skies. Not only have I found my fated one, but her species could save my people.

After the Great Plague swept through our population, we searched the stars for a species that was biologically compatible with ours but found none. Many Drakarians have already resigned themselves to the slow, inevitable extinction of our race. Yet others, like my father, have refused to accept that fate. His conviction is one of the reasons we began negotiating peace with the other Clans. We hoped that encouraging inter-mating between different Clans might help rebuild or at least slow the decline of our numbers.

Happiness brighter than a thousand stars fills me as I turn to my mate, bursting with the knowledge that our future could include fledglings.

Lilliana returns my gaze with confusion etched into her features. "You're a prince?"

I swallow thickly. In all the excitement and anticipation of showing her my home, I forgot to mention my position.

CHAPTER 19

LILLIANA

"You're a prince?" I ask Varus, shocked by Ranas' statement.

Ranas cocks his head to the side as he studies Varus. "You did not tell her?"

"No, he did not." I pull my hand from Varus's grip, glaring at him.

He looks repentant. "I am sorry I did not tell you. I—I thought about sharing but decided not to."

"Why?"

With a heavy sigh, he runs a hand roughly through his hair as he shakes his head. "Because I did not know if you would like me for who I am, not *what* I am. Though few females remain among our people now, many have offered to become my mate. However, I have always known they crave my title and wealth, not my company. My betrothal to the Water Clan Princess was both meant to secure my title and to cement an alliance between our two Clans. I know she does not care for me beyond those gains, just as I do not care about her in that way."

I remember him mentioning a betrothal, but that was before I knew he was a prince and how much this marriage would mean to his people.

I lift my gaze to his. "What happens if you don't go through with the betrothal to the Water Clan Princess? Will that mean war for your people?" I ask because I have to know the answer. Even though I love Varus, I refuse to become the cause of conflict between their Clans.

He takes my hand earnestly. "The alliance was only necessary because our number of females is dwindling. But following the discovery of your people—once we find your females—we will not need such measures. We are biologically compatible. And you said there were several colony ships. We can begin searching for the rest and—"

I pull my hand away and shake my head in disbelief. "So that's what this is all about?"

He cocks his head to the side. "What do you mean?"

"You only want me because your species lacks females. That's the whole reason you want to help us. That's why the Wind Drakarian was so interested in me and why you're in such a hurry to find my people—to keep us all to yourself." I narrow my eyes. "Am I really your fated mate? Or is that just some story you fed me, filling my head with romantic ideas to woo me?"

His mouth drifts open. "I *do* love you, Lilliana. I would not lie about such a thing."

Tears sting my eyes and blur my vision. "How can I know for sure? You've lied so much in the short time that I've known you. How am I supposed to trust your words now?"

I shake my head tenderly. A tear slips down my cheek, but I quickly brush it away. I don't want to cry again.

"All I know is that I've suddenly found out that humans

are the answer to your problems." I lift my gaze to meet his. "I've never been with any other man, Varus. And what happened between us, that was special to me. You're a prince. Like you said, women have been practically falling all over themselves for you, I'm not so naïve as to think the last few days meant as much to you as they did to me. It just… hurts that I gave so much of myself to you and all this time, I don't know if what I thought we had was a lie or not."

Although he is alien, pain is easily read in Varus's features as he stares across at me.

"I don't even know where I am."

Ranas interjects, "You are in the Fire Clan Castle." He clears his throat nervously. "They may be a slightly aggressive Clan, but they are good people. I know this because I have lived among them for many cycles. The prince's intentions are honorable, I assure you."

Although his words sound sincere, I can't forget that he is Varus's friend. Of course, he would call him honorable. I simply don't know what to believe anymore.

I face Varus. "I need some time to think."

He gives me a mournful look. "I will take you to your room."

I nod, reluctantly following him into the hallway. Now that I have a translator chip, I'm painfully aware of every comment his people make about my appearance. My lack of scales, claws, fangs, wings, and so on. From their remarks, I can understand why they believe I am weak.

Panic twists deep in my gut. Physically speaking, my species *is* weaker than theirs. They can shift into monstrous dragons, creatures of old Earth legend. Even if we ask the Drakarians to leave us alone… now that they know we are biologically compatible, what's to stop them from capturing my people? It's not like we could offer much resistance.

When we reach the room that has been prepared for me,

I'm surprised by the spacious layout. A large bed against the far wall draws my attention, a frame of dark wood supporting a floating mattress and rising into a headboard that curves into a partial canopy above. The scarlet comforter looks plush and inviting, embroidered with a symbol I don't recognize. It must be the royal Fire Clan sigil.

Several tapestries decorate the otherwise stark stone walls. Just as the bed hovers off the ground, so do the table and chairs near the balcony. Three large platters of food and a crystal pitcher of water sit on the coffee table and would be tempting if I could muster an appetite right now. Long, flowing curtains of red silk sway in the breeze that drifts in from the balcony nearby. This place is every fairytale fantasy I've ever dreamed up as a child, but suddenly, the sight has become my living nightmare. If I'm not careful, these chambers could easily become my gilded cage.

And yet, when I glance at Varus, I feel conflicted. He's been nothing but kind to me since we met—even before he was sure of our compatibility. Drawing in a deep breath, I force myself to push down all my worries and concerns. I've always been prone to jump to the worst conclusions first. I need time to process my new surroundings and observe objectively.

Varus gestures to a door opposite the balcony. "The cleansing room is through there."

A bath or shower sounds perfect right now. We've been traveling most of the day and I could do with an opportunity to relax and consider the day's events.

Awkwardly, I thank Varus and he steps into the hallway, leaving me alone.

I head straight for the cleansing room, pleasantly surprised to discover an enormous bathing pool carved into the center of the floor.

Dipping my toes into the water, a smile lights my face

when I realize it's already heated. Maybe this pool is like the one in the cave: fed by a warm spring. However, I'm hesitant to get in without first locating a towel or robe, and clothes to change into when I'm clean.

I exit the bathroom and notice another door along the wall. Hopeful that I've found a linen closet, I open it.

My mouth drifts open when I find another room on the other side—with Varus inside.

His head snaps toward me and I hate that my first inclination is to smile before I remember that I'm still mad.

His expression falls as well when I shoot him a wary look. "What is this? Why are you here?"

He blinks several times in confusion. "I gave you my room. The larger one," he adds. "So you would be comfortable."

His answer gives me pause. He's being considerate, as he has been since I first met him. "Thank you," I murmur, ashamed of my initial reaction to finding him here.

Hope crosses his expression and he cautiously steps forward. "May I please explain myself?"

I hold his gaze for a moment before reluctantly nodding my permission.

"When I first saw you, I knew instantly that you were mine. My fated mate. I was shocked because I had never heard of a cross-species mating. And... I'd never seen a human before."

I cross my arms over my chest as I wait for him to continue.

He looks down at his hands. "I wanted so badly to tell you about our bond and my status, but when you described my draka form and I found out how terrified you were, I... simply couldn't form the words. I was afraid you would reject me before you even had a chance to get to know me."

He pauses. "And I desperately wanted you to know me. Not as Prince Varus, but simply as I am.

"Yes, there are few females in my world, but I accepted you without assurance that we would have fledglings. And… I was all right with that. It did not matter to me once I got to know you. Once I saw how brave you were and how kind.

"My people have searched the stars for a species compatible with ours and found nothing. So, I truly believed it would be the same for yours."

I uncross my arms, a challenge in my tone. "And it really didn't matter to you? That we might not be able to have children together?"

He moves closer to take my hand, his eyes never leaving mine. "No. It did not matter. I was already in love with you."

"Now that you know children are possible, how do I know your people won't just want to use humans as breeders?"

His eyes go wide. "We would never do such a thing. Even before the plague swept through our race, females have always been treasured—worshipped. Especially our fated mates." His conviction falters. "There is something else you must know."

"What is it?"

"What happened between us was special to me, too. My people mate for life. I have never been intimate with a female and I refuse to take any other as my mate. If the Water Clan will not release me from my betrothal to their princess, I *will* go to war with them, because I will not take anyone but you as my mate."

"And if I no longer want you?" I ask, because I have to know if his words are true. I have to know that he will not force me or my people to mate with his.

He drops his gaze to the floor, sadness visible in his expression. "I will never force you to be mine if you do not wish it, Lilliana." His green eyes meet mine evenly. "I will keep my promise to help your people. It matters not if they refuse to take mine as mates. No human will ever be forced into anything they do not want."

I rush toward him and wrap my arms around his neck. Stretching onto my toes, I press my lips to his.

When I pull back, his eyes meet mine furtively. "You forgive me?"

I answer without hesitation. "Yes."

A devastatingly handsome grin curves his mouth. He lifts me into his arms, returning my kiss with equal fervor.

"I love you, Lilliana." He smiles against my lips. He walks me back to the cleansing room.

"Let me take care of you, my mate," he murmurs.

CHAPTER 20

LILLIANA

Gently, he sets me down on the edge of the pool and slowly begins to undress me. He dips his hands beneath the hem of my shirt and pulls the fabric over my head, discarding it on the floor beside me.

His eyes meet mine. "We will not do anything until you are ready," he assures me softly. "I merely want to take care of you. My instincts demand that I make certain you are safe, warm, and happy, my linaya."

He carefully pulls me into the water beside him as he runs a cloth over my body. He pulls me into his lap, kneading the muscles along my neck and shoulders, and I relax against him, enjoying the feel of his strong hands.

My worries slowly melt away beneath his ministrations as I close my eyes and allow my thoughts to float to the surface of my mind untethered.

I've always had a plan for my life. An idea of what I thought my future would be. I chose my profession to help people; I wanted to be someone who could both serve and lead. That's why I ventured into the desert by myself the day I met Varus. I've never backed down from a challenge, so when we landed on this desolate planet, I was determined to take risks to survive and ensure the survival of my people.

The colony ships were never supposed to land here. And yet, fate brought us to Drakaria and delivered me into the arms of a caring, attentive man. Isn't that what I've always wanted in a partner—someone who cares for me as much as I do for him?

As his hands run soothingly up and down my back, desire pools deep in my core. I want him. But his people mate for life. I have to be sure before we take the next step.

I pull back just enough to meet his reflective green eyes. "You say we are fated, but are you certain that you love me?" My voice is barely a whisper as I wait with anxiety and anticipation for his answer.

He leans forward and touches his forehead to mine, closing his eyes briefly before opening them to send me a look of intense love and devotion. "You are fierce, brave, intelligent, kind, and beautiful. Everything I could ever wish for in a mate. I will never love another as I love you, Lilliana. Please accept me as yours."

My heart squeezes painfully in my chest at his vulnerable expression. I wrap my arms around his neck and press my lips to his. He opens his mouth and my tongue curls around his, deepening our kiss.

He locks his arms around my waist and pulls me forward until I'm straddling his lap. His stav is a hard bar between us, resting against my inner thigh. His scales are soft like silk against my skin as I trace my hands over the muscles of his abdomen and chest, memorizing the hard planes of muscle beneath the tips of my fingers.

I've never made love before, but already I ache, longing to

take him deep inside me. I roll my hips against his and he groans low in his throat.

He grips my left thigh, careful of his claws as he kneads the tender flesh. He runs his other hand gently over my hair. Grasping the strands between his fingers, he tips my head up, his gaze fiery and possessive.

He slants his lips over mine, spearing his tongue into my mouth as he claims me with a branding kiss. "Mine," he growls low in his throat, sending shivers of pleasure through my body.

"Yours," I agree as I return his kiss with equal fervor.

My entire body aches with pent up need. I want him inside me, but I've never done this before. I've always heard that the first time can be painful. I'm starting to lose my nerve.

Sensing my hesitance, he pulls back. He cups his hand to the back of my neck and rubs the soft pad of his thumb across my cheek. "We do not have to mate if you are not ready, my Lilliana."

Heat flushes my cheeks. "I—It's just that I've never done this before and I... don't know what I'm doing," I admit shyly.

He takes my hand, guiding it to his hardened length between us. He's so large, my fingers don't quite reach as I try to wrap them around his girth. I study his stav, noting all the ways he is different from every image I've ever seen of a human man.

His erection is ridged with soft, textured scales. He inhales sharply as I run my hand along his length before placing the head against the entrance of my core. "You are certain?" he rasps.

"Yes, Varus. I want you." I press my lips to his.

His gaze holds mine as he slowly enters my channel. Tight heat blooms inside me and I gasp. He goes completely still, waiting for my body to adjust to his invasion. "Are you all right?" he asks, worry written across his features.

I nod, then carefully lower myself until his stav is completely sheathed inside me. Gently, he rolls his hips against mine. My head falls back, and a soft moan escapes my lips as the textured scales of his stav create the most delicious friction deep in my channel.

With one arm around my waist, his other hand grips my hip to hold me close as he begins to stroke into me. At first, his movements are slow and shallow, allowing my body to adjust.

Small shivers of pleasure ripple through me and I moan into his mouth. "More, Varus."

His gaze holds mine as he pulls back and thrusts into me. My mouth falls open and his name leaves my lips in a breathless sigh.

He changes the angle of his hips, sinking impossibly deeper. Never did I imagine my first time would be like this. Every inch of my skin is sensitive and each movement of his stav inside me brings new pleasure.

His strokes become longer and deeper. I get lost in the sensation of our bodies moving as one. Nothing exists beyond this moment with him. Desire coils tightly in my core with each thrust of his hips up into mine.

Intense heat bursts inside me and I inhale sharply at the overwhelming and delicious sensation. "What is that?" I barely manage.

He growls low in his chest, clenching his jaw as he struggles to maintain his control. "My precum to soften and open your womb, preparing you to accept my essence. I will fill you so full of my seed that every male within several arcums will know you are mine, and that I have claimed you. I will take you many times this night, my linaya."

His words ignite desire deep inside me. The small

muscles of my channel quiver and flex around his length as he picks up his pace, pulling me toward the edge as I chase my release. He growls as his rhythm begins to stutter, then he thrusts deep, setting off a cascade of intense pleasure that washes through me as I reach my climax and stars explode behind my eyes.

He holds me close in an almost crushing embrace and I surrender myself completely as his length begins to pulse deep inside me. He roars my name as a wave of intense warmth erupts from his stav as he fills me with his essence, triggering another orgasm even stronger than the last as his seed floods my womb.

His stav is still buried deep inside me as he captures my mouth in a branding kiss. I cup his cheek and he drops his forehead to mine, closing his eyes as he inhales deeply.

"You are mine, Lilliana," he whispers. "My beautiful mate."

"And you're mine," I reply, relaxing in his embrace.

I gasp and moan as he begins moving his hips against mine.

"I need you again," he rasps.

I hold him close, arching into his every stroke as I'm swept away into blissful pleasure.

CHAPTER 21

LILLIANA

In the morning, I wake to his head between my thighs. I look down to find his eyes on me as he runs his tongue through my soft folds, gently teasing the sensitive bud of flesh at the apex.

My head falls back, and a soft moan escapes my lips. I reach for him, gripping his horns, urging him to continue.

I comb my hands through his hair, grasping the silky strands between my fingers as he relentlessly laps at my folds. He presses a finger into my channel, once again teasing his tongue over the sensitive bundle of nerves, and I cry out his name as pleasure ripples through me.

I gently tug at his hair, pulling his body up so his face is even with mine. I open my thighs to cradle his hips and gasp as the head of his stav slowly begins to enter me.

With each movement of his hips, he strokes long and deep inside me until I'm breathless and panting beneath him. I run my hands down his back, feeling his strong muscles flex beneath my fingers as he thrusts deep into me.

He stares down at me, his dark green eyes full of love. He captures my mouth with his own. I wrap my arms and legs tightly around him and he groans low in his throat. "You are mine, Lilliana."

"Yours," I agree in a breathless whisper as he erupts deep inside me, filling me with his seed. My release follows his and I cry out his name as wave after wave of pleasure moves through my body.

When he doesn't pull away but instead begins to stroke deep within me again, I consider telling him to stop; that I need to rest. My entire body is sore, especially between my thighs. My muscles tremble slightly as I wrap my legs around him, unaccustomed to maintaining this position for as long as they did last night. However, when he quickens his pace and begins to thrust long and deep, a low moan escapes me. I love the delicious friction of his ridged stav deep in my channel, hitting me in all the right places and driving my pleasure to new heights.

My toes begin to curl, already anticipating my next release. I love the sensation of his strong, muscular body covering mine.

I want him—all of him.

I cry out, digging my nails into his back as he grips my hips firmly, pinning me to the mattress. He roars my name as he erupts deep inside me, filling me again with the delicious warmth of his seed.

Panting heavily, he collapses. He carefully keeps his weight balanced on his elbows on either side of me to avoid crushing me. I'm surprised not only at his stamina but also at how he's able to remain inside me after he has found his release. I've heard human men can't do this, and I strongly doubt that human men could make love as many consecutive times as we did last night.

I wrap my arms around him and hold him close, enjoying the masculine spice and cinnamon scent that is distinctly his.

He nuzzles my neck, running his tongue along the pulsing artery.

"You are addicting," he whispers against my skin. "I could take you all day and all night and still want more."

Running my fingers tenderly through the short hairs at the nape of his neck, I feel the same.

CHAPTER 22

VARUS

I hold Lilliana close. With my stav still buried deep in her channel, I nuzzle her neck and inhale deeply of the combined scent of our mating. Her inner thighs are sticky with my release and yet, I find myself wanting to take her once more, desiring more than anything for my seed to take root deep within her womb. I can hardly believe that I am holding my linaya in my arms.

As my gaze travels over her smaller form, I release a deep sigh of contentment. Her name stands for a flower on her home world, I remember. She is as beautiful as the inora flower and her features, while just as delicate, hide a strength of will that rivals any Drakarian female.

I roll to the side until we are facing one another. She nestles against my form and I tug her close as myriad thoughts float to the surface of my mind.

I must officially break off my betrothal to Noralla and I must do so delicately. I do not want to instigate a war between our two Clans, one that could drag Lilliana's people into it as well. The Wind Clan has already become our enemy since Raidyn broke our treaty. My Clan cannot afford to fight a war on two fronts.

But one question remains: what do I do about Lilliana's people?

Should I tell the Water Clan about the humans or would it be wiser to keep their species a secret?

Lilliana tips her head back to meet my eyes with a sleepy smile. She runs her hand tenderly over the scales on my chest and abdomen as she gives me a questioning look. "What's wrong, Varus?"

"I was thinking of the Water Clan princess."

Her expression falters and she stills.

Recognizing the beginnings of devastation written in her features, I move to reassure her. "I do not regret binding myself to you. I was merely thinking of how I left the betrothal ceremony without officially canceling the agreement with Noralla. If we are to avoid war with their people over a broken betrothal, I must speak to her and explain what has happened."

Lilliana nods in understanding. "I don't want to be the reason your people go to war, Varus."

"Even if we did," I whisper, "I would not regret taking you as mine." I pause. "But I am uncertain if I should tell them about you... or your people. Raidyn of the Wind Clan already saw you and I believe it is only a matter of time before the other Clans discover the truth as well. I think it would be wise to share with the Water Clan now, rather than wait for them to hear it elsewhere."

"I think you're right; sooner or later, everyone will find out. You can't keep us a secret for long." She gently pushes me onto my back, resting her chin on my chest as her luminous green eyes meet mine. "Tell Noralla that you found your fated mate. Tell her people about mine. But only if you believe they won't hunt us like the Wind Clan."

"Whatever happens, my Clan will protect yours," I reassure her. "In becoming my mate, you are granted the title of future Fire Queen. As such, your people fall under our protection."

She still looks uncertain. "You really don't think the Water Clan will react aggressively like the Wind Clan did?"

"No. I do not."

She smiles. "Then, let's go talk to them. The sooner we finish, the sooner we can retrieve my people."

I wrap my arms around her, hugging her close to my chest as I run my fingers through her long, silken red hair.

"What's wrong?" she whispers.

"It is instinct," I tell her. "Possessiveness of one's mate."

She moans softly as I cup her breast and kiss a heated trail down the elegant curve of her neck. I will make love to her again before we speak with the Water Clan. Instinct demands that I fill her with my essence so that every unbonded male knows without a doubt that she is mine. "I must have you again, my beautiful linaya."

Dressed in the silken robes of our people, Lilliana stands beside me as I summon my faithful guard and friend, Rakan. We grew up together, he and I. With orange-red scales and crimson eyes, he stands tall and proud before us for a moment before bowing low to my mate.

As he straightens, I do not miss the way his gaze rakes over her features in fascination. A low growl rumbles in my chest and Lilliana places a hand on my forearm. I turn to find her smiling.

"You really need to stop doing that, Varus. I'm yours, my love. I don't want anyone else."

Her words fill me with pride as I turn back to face my friend.

"Rakan?"

"Yes, my prince?"

"I need your oath that you will protect and defend my mate, who is more precious to me than all the world. Swear that you will protect our future—the future queen of our Clan."

"I swear, my prince," he bows low again. "I will protect the princess with my life."

I place a hand on his shoulder and meet his eyes evenly. "Thank you, my friend."

He dips his chin in a subtle nod and I turn to face Lilliana. "Please, my mate, wait here while I go speak with the Water Clan."

"Shouldn't I go with you?"

I shake my head softly. "I do not want them to know of your existence until I am certain they are not a threat."

CHAPTER 23

VARUS

My footsteps echo as I enter the throne room. My mother's hard gaze falls upon me. Noralla and her brother, Prince Llyr, stand off to the side, observing my approach with curious expressions.

I have only talked with Noralla and Llyr a few times since our betrothal was announced. They are twins, nearly identical. With scales the color of the crystal-clear oceans and silver eyes, their elegant features and the regal set of the aquamarine horns spiraling from their heads give them a proud appearance. Guilt fills me as they turn to me now with questioning eyes.

Llyr's nostrils flare when I move closer and Noralla's brows furrow. Even though they would not recognize her species, they can scent my mate. I should have washed the evidence of our mating from my body, but my primal instincts demanded that I remain covered in her scent so that all would know I am fully mated and have claimed Lilliana as mine.

Llyr steps forward. "What is the meaning of this? Why did you miss the betrothal ceremony? Where have you been?"

It doesn't escape me that his expression shows more concern than anger. This is good. Perhaps the Water Clan will be open to maintaining our alliance even without a royal mating.

"Forgive me," I begin. "I flew into the desert before the ceremony and was caught in a sandstorm."

Noralla appears equally concerned. She moves toward me, worry etched into her features. "But you are well now, are you not?"

My hearts clench. I have wronged this female and I am ashamed that I did not think to speak with her the moment I returned.

"Yes," I reply. "But..." I hesitate, uncertain of how to continue. Drawing in a deep breath to steady my nerves, I meet her eyes evenly. "There is something else you must know."

She blinks. "What is it?"

"When I was out in the desert, I found my fated one—my linaya." I pause. "Forgive me, but I cannot go through with our betrothal."

Something akin to relief crosses her features. I would be offended if I had not been the one to call off our bonding. She darts a glance at her brother; his expression mirrors hers.

"I understand," she replies. "A fated bond is sacred, blessed by the Gods themselves. It cannot be ignored once found."

Llyr steps forward. "I would be lying if I said this news did not please me."

I gape at him. Am I really such a terrible match for his sister?

"It would have grieved me to say goodbye to my sister

after your bonding. We are close, she and I. I admit that I dreaded the thought of having to leave her behind."

She smiles warmly at me. "Do not be offended, Varus. You are a good male, but I am of the Water Clan. I do not believe my people are suited to your desert climate."

Llyr nods in agreement. "This does not mean, however, that we will disregard the peace agreement we agreed upon between our people."

Relief fills me at their words. A glance at my parents tells me they feel the same.

Llyr arches a brow. "Who is the female the Gods have chosen for you?"

Silence greets his question as I struggle to formulate an answer that does not reveal my mate's race. However, I realize that my Clan's newfound alliance with the Water Clan should not begin with an act of deception.

"She is not Drakarian," I finally say.

He frowns. "Not Drakarian? Then... what is she?"

"A race we have never encountered before. They are called humans and they hail from a planet called Earth."

"Humans?" Noralla repeats the word quietly to herself. "I have never heard of Earth before. Are they part of the Galactic Federation of Planets?"

I shake my head and the siblings' eyes widen slightly. They are too polite to ask further questions. Many species have petitioned to join the Federation but were denied for being too primitive. I'm sure they believe this is the reason her species is not a member.

How do I know this? Because it was the same conclusion I reached when I first realized Lilliana did not have a translator chip. My mate is not primitive, however, and I am eager to introduce her to the Water Clan so they may see this for themselves. She is as brilliant as she is beautiful, and I am proud to call her mine.

It is easy to see that Noralla and Llyr have many questions, and I plan on answering them to the best of my ability, but first, they must meet my Lilliana.

"I will send for my mate," I tell them, turning to one of the guards, who rushes to retrieve her.

An awkward silence hangs in the air as we anxiously wait for her to appear. I know the moment she enters because Llyr's mouth drifts open as she walks toward us with Rakan at her side.

She takes my hand, entwining our fingers before she looks up at me with a dazzling smile.

I gesture to Llyr and Noralla. "This is Princess Noralla and Prince Llyr of the Water Clan." I turn to my mate. "And this is Lilliana of Earth, my linaya. Her people are under the protection of the Fire Clan."

Llyr blinks several times. "There are more of her kind?"

I nod, noting the question he doesn't voice. Like every Drakarian who has met my mate, he is wondering if her species is biologically compatible with ours.

Lilliana looks up at him. "Our ship crashed in the desert plains. We did not realize this planet was already inhabited. I was out testing soil samples to begin cultivating crops when Varus rescued me from a predator." She sighs heavily. "But my people probably believe me dead since I haven't returned for days." Her eyes dart to me, then back to Llyr and Noralla. "We are going to find them and bring them back to live with the Fire Clan."

"When I was in the desert with my mate, searching for her people, Prince Raidyn of the Wind Clan saw her. And he saw this." I gesture to the glowing pattern of scales upon my chest, indicating Lilliana is my fated one.

Llyr's eyes widen slightly. "It is truth," he mutters. "The Gods have gifted you with the fated bond."

"Yes, I recognized it immediately when I came upon her

in the desert." I pause. "When Raidyn saw this mark, he attacked me."

"I thought your two Clans had a treaty of nonaggression between you."

"We did," my father interjects. "Raidyn has broken the alliance by attacking my son."

Llyr nods and lowers his gaze with a pensive look before facing me. "They are probably hunting the humans already," he says, concern etched into his features. "My people can help you search, if you will accept."

I bite back a low growl as fierce possessiveness moves through me. Logically, I understand this is an effect of our mating bond, but all reason abandons me when Llyr's gaze rakes up and down Lilliana's form with intense fascination evident in his eyes. I'm certain she appears more attractive to him now, despite the lack of scales, wings, and natural defenses. For he has seen proof of the fated bond between us.

I wonder if this deeply possessive instinct will ever truly fade. Surely it must. I cannot imagine spending the rest of my life ready to fight and kill every male that even looks Lilliana's way.

"That will not be necessary," I tell him. "We have enough warriors to search for her Clan."

He nods, but I read the disappointment in his expression. More females would be a blessing to his Clan, as well.

CHAPTER 24

LILLIANA

Both Llyr and Noralla's eyes weigh heavily on me as they rake over my form.

I suppose I must be a curious sight to behold. Varus said that ours is the first interspecies fated mate bond. In Llyr's expression, I notice a strange mixture of hope and disbelief. I expected Noralla might be jealous that I took her fiancé, but I see nothing but intense fascination in her gaze.

Prince Llyr steps forward, brow furrowed. "How does your kind protect itself? You do not seem to have any natural defenses."

Varus snarls at the comment even though he's admitted to thinking the same thing. I suppose he feels differently now that I'm his mate, but I'm not offended in the least.

"We wear protective clothing and use weapons to defend ourselves," I explain.

Llyr nods with a pensive look. "Is it true there are more of you? More females?"

In his eyes, I can read hope. If the plague Varus told me

about affected all the Clans, women must be as precious as they are rare on this planet.

"Yes. There were twenty-five of us total on the escape pod, including five men. There were many more humans on our colony ships, but we haven't managed to locate any other survivors yet."

Both Llyr and Rakan inhale sharply at my statement.

"A gift from the Gods," Llyr whispers under his breath. He turns to Varus. "You cannot mean to keep them hidden from the rest of the Clans, can you?"

Indignation fills me as I interrupt. "My people escaped our dying home world. We were hunted down by pirates and somehow managed to survive crash-landing on this planet. We are not about to become breeders for your people just because you lack women."

He blinks several times, dumbfounded. "We would never do such a thing," he denies vehemently. "Females are cherished and treasured. None would ever be forced to carry fledglings against her will. My vow." He bows slightly and then straightens. "Forgive me. I meant no offense. I meant to say, what if there are others beyond the Fire Clan who are fated to a human, just as Varus was fated to be yours?"

I back down, ashamed that I jumped to conclusions. "No, Llyr. Forgive me for accusing you of ill intent." I gently squeeze Varus's hand. "My mate told me that your people would never mistreat a female. I suppose after the pirate attack, it's hard for me to realize that not everyone is out to harm us."

He frowns. "What did these pirates who attacked your ship look like?"

I look him up and down. "They had scales like your people, and a long, tapered tail, sharp claws, and fangs. No wings, though."

His eyes widen, as do Noralla's. Llyr's gaze snaps toward

Varus. "We need to send out ships to search for any other survivors of their ships, as soon as possible."

Varus nods. "I agree. The Rovarans are ruthless mercenaries and slavers." He looks to me. "Your species is similar to the Elveron; one female would sell for thousands of credits in the slave trade."

"You must let our Clan help yours in the search for your mate's people," Llyr tells Varus. "Before it is too late."

I turn to Llyr. "I appreciate your concern for my people, but I need to make sure you understand something first."

He cocks his head to the side. "What is it?"

"Your species believe mine are gifts from the Gods. And while that may be true, we are also just people—sentient beings, just like you. We are survivors trying to forge a new life now that our home world is gone. You need to understand that not every human woman will be open to the idea of bonding to one of your men." I glance at Varus. "I love Varus, but I did not experience the instant recognition he did when he first saw me. My species does not experience fated bonds as yours does. I hope that we can build an alliance with your race. One that is forged in peace, mutual understanding, and respect."

He dips his chin in a subtle nod. "That is my hope as well, Princess."

CHAPTER 25

LILLIANA

We stand on the balcony of the main floor of the castle. I turn my gaze toward the desert plains. The red sands are as vast as an ocean and extend as far as the eye can see. My people are out there, waiting for us to find them.

Little do they know I'm bringing them both salvation and a future I'm not sure they're ready to embrace. We always assumed we'd colonize an uninhabited world and start over fresh. We weren't prepared to deal with another sentient species, even though we suspected before we left that aliens existed somewhere in the dark void of space.

We're surrounded by over a dozen warriors of the Fire Clan. All of them are unclothed, like Varus, and preparing to shift into draka form. While I know nudity is not frowned upon by his people, I can't help but think mine are going to be astounded not only by real-life dragons but also when those same dragons shift into a group of naked Drakarian men before their eyes.

Varus growls low in his throat and when I turn to him with a questioning look, he wraps a possessive arm around me. "You are mine and mine alone."

At first, I don't understand the cause of his jealousy, but then I realize he's reacting to my visual appraisal of his warriors. I smile, squeezing his hand. "I'm yours," I agree, watching the fiery possessiveness leave his eyes.

Ranas explained this is a part of Varus' mating heat. That his protective instincts are heightened in response to some strange compulsion of his biology during the fertile peak of my cycle. With as many times as we've made love, I'd be worried about getting pregnant if Ranas hadn't assured me some medical intervention would likely be required for that to happen.

It's not that I don't want children with Varus. It's just that we're still in the early stages of our official bonding and I'd like some more time to ourselves before we have fledglings, as Varus' people refer to them.

Satisfied with my answer, a smile crests Varus' lips. He gives me a tender kiss before turning to face his warriors again.

I tilt my chin up as I address the men assembled before me. "When we find my people, you must realize what a shock our arrival may be to them. We have not had much contact with other species outside of our own ever since we set out on the colony ships from our world." I pause, allowing my gaze to drift over each warrior before I continue. "There is also the chance that my people may not wish to return with us to the city. I will do my best to convince them, but ultimately, it is their decision to come with us or not."

Rakan steps forward, seeming concerned. "But surely they must realize they'd be safer within our city than out on the desert plains?"

I nod. "That is my hope as well, but their agreement is not assured. That's why I must convince them. But until I do, you must follow my lead so that they do not view your race as a threat."

Rakan bows low and then straightens.

Varus steps forward, turning a hard gaze on all his warriors. "I know each of you carries the hope that you will find your fated one among the females as I did. But you must remember that the fate bond does not present itself to them as it does to us. They will not recognize it. You must not approach the females too eagerly, lest you scare them away. Do you understand?"

Each warrior nods in agreement.

"Now, assemble the wing!" he commands, and I watch as they fall into formation behind us.

With a sudden whirl of dust and wind, Varus transforms into a fierce and beautiful draka. He turns his massive head to me and gives me his best attempt at a draka smile before crouching and extending his leg so I can climb on.

I'm nervous to mount him in front of his men since I've only technically done this twice. Carefully, I clamber up his leg and settle onto his back, between his shoulders.

Without warning, Varus leaps from the balcony. He extends his wings to catch the wind like billowing sails, flapping furiously as we ascend into the sky.

Dipping his wing to the left, he banks in a long, slow arc over the castle grounds. I watch, enthralled, as each of his warriors shifts and takes flight from the balcony as well. I realize this is why Varus is circling the palace grounds—he's waiting for each of his warriors to transform before leading them across the plains.

I scan the area around us, amazed at how many Drakarians are in flight over the city, down by the river, and above the farmlands below. I also see many in humanoid form, walking along the streets, milling around various stores, and shopping at open-air markets as they go about their day. Some are clothed in long, silken, colorful robes like mine, but most of them are nude.

I can hardly wait to explore the city, but there will be plenty of time for that later. Right now, our priority is finding my people and bringing them to safety. Even if the Wind Clan doesn't find them, the desert is rife with predators and sandstorms. Despite our years of training to adapt to a new world, I know we're not ready for those dangers.

Varus folds his wings and we dive down the side of the mesa, leaving the castle behind and heading toward the river below. He skims one claw across the water, and I watch in wonder as our image ripples and distorts along the reflective surface.

Once we've crossed to the other shore, his wings billow like great sails beating furiously and we climb again. The wind whips violently around my form, trying to pull me off his back, but I hold tightly to his spikes. Once, I would have been afraid, but I know Varus would never let me fall. I trust him. Completely.

As we reach the top of the plateau just beyond the water, I marvel at the vast expanse of the desert that spreads out ahead. Crimson waves of sand dotted by several towering rock formations like bare islands amid the desert sea.

The sun beats down relentlessly overhead, but the winds whipping around us keep me cool enough for comfort. I raise the hood of my robe over my head, shielding my eyes from the worst of the sun's rays.

Varus has assured me the journey to where he first found me won't be long, but as far as I'm concerned, we can't reach my people fast enough. I think of Anna, Talia, Milo, and Skye. They probably think I'm dead.

I can't wait to show them what I've found and introduce them to Varus. I rest my chin lovingly against his back. I love this man and I'm eager for him to meet my friends. Moreover, I am desperate to get my loved ones to safety.

Stars forbid the Wind Clan captures them first.

CHAPTER 26

VARUS

I lead our formation back toward the site where I found
Lilliana. She is uncertain where exactly her people have
settled but suspects they are nearby since the rover she
used to reach that area has a limited range.

My mate chastises herself for not possessing a better
sense of direction, but I reassure her that this is something
that could just as easily happen to a Drakarian. The harsh
winds of the desert plains are constantly shifting the dunes,
making it impossible to identify landmarks, especially after a
sandstorm.

A flash of light in the distance catches my eye. Lilliana
must notice it too because she taps my shoulder and cries out
in excitement. "Over there! That's our ship!"

As one, our group turns in that direction. Rakan flies up
beside me, projecting concern. He is probably thinking the
same as me—the humans are dangerously close to Wind
Clan territory. If I had to guess, they must have crashed right
along the border between the Fire and Wind lands. It's highly

likely they've already been discovered by Prince Raidyn's people. I only hope that I am wrong.

As we approach, small figures begin scrambling for cover below. It is just as Lilliana predicted—the sight of my brethren is frightening to her kind—but it cannot be helped. Until we land, we must maintain this form.

A female wails in terror as we set down upon the ground. "It's one of the monsters that stole Skye!"

My hearts stop. It is as I'd feared. They have already been discovered by another Clan.

In a whirl of dust and sand, we shift one by one as our feet touch the ground, Lilly jumping to the ground beside me. Gasps sound from several of the humans as they watch us warily from behind pitiful hiding places: boxes, crates, pieces of their wrecked ship, and such. Do they really believe such poor shelters will keep them safe? They are in dire need of protection. I can only hope they accept our offer to provide it.

Lilliana takes my hand in her own. One of the braver females emerges from behind part of the wrecked ship as soon as she notices my mate. "Lilliana, is that you?"

My mate smiles in greeting. "Yes, Talia, it's me."

This female is brave indeed, for she runs up to Lilliana, ignoring the ring of warriors surrounding her. She throws her arms around her and hugs her tightly. "Oh my Stars! We thought you were dead!"

"No, I'm fine, I swear," Lilliana soothes her, then turns to me. "This is my… husband, Varus."

Husband? This is the first time she has used that term, but according to my translator, she has called me her mate.

The female's jaw drops as wide, blue eyes turn to me. "Husband? Him? An alien dragon man?"

I purse my lips in slight annoyance. I suppose *alien dragon man* is better than *ugly lizard man*, as Lilliana first called me after I rescued her.

She nods, glancing over the female's shoulder to scan the rest of her people, who are slowly creeping out from behind their poorly sheltered hiding places. "Where's Skye?"

Skye. I heard that name as we were landing. I forget that my mate's hearing is not as acute as mine.

Talia gives her a grim look. "She was taken by one of them." She raises her hand, pointing an accusing finger at Rakan.

Offended, he growls low in his throat. "I would never steal a female."

Talia's face pales at the guttural sound of our language. I forgot that my mate's people lack translator chips. Fortunately, my mate remembers.

"He says he would never steal a female," she translates.

"That—that's what he said?" Her friend's voice quavers slightly as she studies Rakan in wide-eyed fear.

I meet her gaze. "No male of the Fire Clan would," I state firmly, then look to my mate. "Please tell her this."

"How do you understand their language?" her friend asks, curiosity slipping into her tone.

Lilliana taps the space behind her left ear where her translator chip is embedded beneath the skin.

"They have translator chips." She grins. "They can give one to all of you."

I am pleased when the female relaxes slightly. We are already beginning to establish the beginnings of trust with my mate's friends.

Talia turns to a human male. At least, that's what I assume he is. If this creature is female, she is hideous, lacking the soft curves and delicate form of my mate and many of the other humans that have gathered around. He is square jawed, covered in a light smattering of coarse, dark fur, and smells as if he has rolled around in a carcass that has been dead for several days. I certainly hope this person is male, for I know he will never find a mate among any of the Clans otherwise.

"John was with her when she was taken. He saw the dragon that took her."

She called him "he," so I surmise that my appraisal was correct. This foul-smelling, hideous creature is a male of their species. I dart a glance at my warriors and tilt my chin up with pride. If these human males are our rivals, they do not stand a chance. My people are by far more handsome and definitely cleaner.

I note that several human females are already staring at me and my warriors with something akin to wonder. Several of the males behind me puff their chests out, displaying their muscular forms as they would to a Drakarian female.

"Ask her to describe this dragon's appearance," I tell my mate, anxiously awaiting her answer.

I suspect it was a member of the Wind Clan, and if so, we will have trouble retrieving the stolen female from them.

The creature—John—steps forward, tipping his chin up. His gaze rakes over my form, expression caught between disbelief and disgust.

I arch a brow in response, for the feeling is mutual.

John narrows his eyes. "It was an ugly bastard, just like them," he also points at Rakan, who snarls at the accusation. "A hideous monster."

I purse my lips, barely able to suppress the menacing growl that rumbles in my chest. How dare this filthy creature call *us* hideous? Perhaps he is possessed of even poorer sight than my mate and cannot see how pitiful he is compared to a Drakarian male. "Ask him what color his scales were."

Lilliana repeats my question.

"Light gray," he replies, and my hearts stop. I was right—a

member of the Wind Clan has kidnapped Skye. This is deeply troubling, to say the least.

I approach him and he takes a step back, stumbling slightly. It seems he is not as brave as he tries to appear in front of the females. I am doubly glad we found these females; their pitiful human males are obviously unable to protect such precious treasures.

"The Drakarian who took her is part of the Wind Clan. That coloring is specific to their people." I hold his gaze with confidence. "What else can you tell us about him? Any markings?"

I wait patiently for my mate to relay my words.

John brings his hand to his jaw, massaging the small tuft of coarse brown fur on his chin as he lifts a thoughtful gaze to the sky. "Yeah. He had a long scar on the left side of his monstrous face."

My eyes widen and so do Rakan's beside me.

"It was Raidyn," I conclude, and my warriors all nod in agreement.

Most of our Clan knows of the scar that mars Raidyn's face. It is the reason he has been passed over by many females and unable to procure a mate despite his status as prince. Drakarian females are vain and only want a perfect, unblemished male.

I believe this also explains his gruff demeanor. If our situations were reversed, I suspect I'd be bitter, as well. It must be difficult to be judged so harshly for a superficial flaw.

I turn to the creature, John. "Do not be afraid. No Drakarian, no matter what Clan, would ever harm a female."

Lilliana relays my words and then poses the most important question. "Varus is the prince of the Fire Clan. They have offered to take us all back to their city for protection, if you're willing to come."

John narrows his eyes and steps in front of Talia. "I don't

trust them." He grits through his teeth. "They could be luring us into a trap."

My mate huffs out a frustrated breath and places her hands on her hips as she levels a dark gaze at the male.

"Look at them." She gestures to me and my warriors. "I mean, take a really good look."

I'm surprised to note intense fascination rather than fear on many of the human female's faces as their eyes scan my warriors. It is almost as if they are appraising them like a female Drakarian would when considering a mate. I do not doubt that most of my warriors, if not all, will be able to find a mate among Lilliana's people, if the female's interested stares are any indication.

Sensing their gazes, I notice my warriors straightening their stances, standing tall and proud. A few of them even shift to display their flexing muscles, demonstrating their strength to the pool of available females.

Lilliana continues. "Look how strong they are."

My warriors snap to attention, tipping their chins higher with pride at her words.

"If they wanted to take us, they could. There would be nothing we could do about it." She pauses, allowing the weight of her words to settle. "But they haven't harmed us. Instead, they are asking us to come live in their city. A city with running water, technology, and amenities. They are offering protection, in case the pirates come looking for us."

A few of the human's eyes widen with fear at her last statement. One of them speaks up. "You think they'll come searching for us here? Even without the transmitter beacon?"

I nod. "Yes. The pirates who attacked you are known as mercenaries and slavers. They would not give up their quarry so easily. But under the protection of the Fire Clan, we would be safe."

When Lilliana relays my statement, many of the females

huddle closer as if already instinctively turning to my warriors for safety. This is excellent. They already regard my people as allies instead of enemies—and someday, I hope, as potential mates.

"But what about the dragon who took Skye? Why did he take her?"

Her question is one I've been turning over in my mind ever since Talia explained what happened. I do not know why he did this, especially if the female was unwilling. There must be more to the story than what has been shared so far. I narrow my eyes and face John.

"Were you in any type of danger when Raidyn came upon you?"

He swallows thickly and lowers his gaze as if my question disturbs him.

"I..." He clears his throat nervously. "I mean, we... we weren't in any danger at the time."

My nostrils flare at the acrid scent of fear that begins to seep from his pores. There is something he is not telling us. "What are you hiding?" I demand.

He sends me a nervous look as Lilliana translates my question. Clearing his throat again, he shakes his head vehemently. "Nothing. I'm not hiding anything. I've already told you what happened." His gaze shifts to my mate. "We were out looking for you when the dragon took her."

Something about his statement troubles me. I doubt his words are truth. From Lilliana's expression, it is easy to see that she suspects this, too.

John glares at me and then turns to face his people. "I think we should stay here and take our chances in the desert rather than entrust our lives to these monsters."

With a frustrated sigh, I arch a brow at my mate. "He does realize we can understand everything he is saying, does he not?"

She rolls her eyes, shaking her head before addressing her people. "I know it seems scary to entrust our lives to a bunch of aliens. Ones that can shift into dragons, at that. But," she takes my hand and entwines our fingers, holding them up for her people to see, "Varus rescued me from a predator that would have killed me in the desert. He has done nothing but take care of me since then."

She turns her gaze to my warriors. "I cannot speak for the Wind Clan, but I can tell you that the Fire Clan are good people. And they are willing to welcome us into their city and offer us a new, safe life." Her eyes drift over their pitiful settlement. "Besides, our chance of survival is much better with them than out here in the desert."

Several murmurs of agreement follow her statement. One by one, the females step forward. Four more males join John, standing beside him, three of them leveling a dark gaze at me and my warriors. It seems they are not happy with this turn of events, but they are pitifully outnumbered.

As my gaze rakes over their forms, it is easy to see how much taller and stronger my people are compared to human males. No wonder these females do not feel protected. Their males are weak.

Talia turns to the others. "This calls for a vote. How many are in favor of going with Lilliana and her..." She turns to me with a nervous smile before looking back at her people, "her mate... er... husband?"

All the females raise their hands and all but one of the males do not. It is official. They have lost the vote and I care not if they decide to stay behind. Especially the one named John.

Mistrust shines in the males' eyes, but I suppose I would be protective of the females as well in their place. In truth, I should not fault them. As pitiful as they may be, they are obviously trying their best to appear strong and capable.

I face Lilliana. "It is decided, then. Each human will go with one of my warriors to fly back to the city."

After she relays the message, my men begin to shift form. Several of the females and a few of the males inhale sharply as they watch.

My mate places a hand on my forearm, drawing my attention back to her. "What about Skye? We have to get her back, Varus."

"We will," I tell her. "But first, we must return to the city."

Her worried eyes remain locked on mine and I reach out to cup her cheek. "I vow to you, my beautiful mate, Raidyn and his people would never harm a female. She is safe." I turn a dark gaze toward John. "I suspect there is more to the story of how she was taken than that male is telling us."

She narrows her eyes. "I get the same feeling."

"We will send an ambassador to the Wind Clan to find out why she was taken and to ask for her return."

Lilliana nods.

As we fly back in formation, I note several of my warriors seem pleased with the female on their backs. I wonder if any of them have identified their fated mate, as I did when I first saw Lilliana.

The ghost of a smile seems permanently frozen onto Rakan's normally stoic face while we cross the desert, heading back to the city.

I will ask my father to offer Lilliana's Clan all the rights granted to our people so that they may live among us as equals. Whatever the future holds, we will now face it together—as one people instead of two.

EPILOGUE

Lilliana

    Although it feels like I've known Varus forever, it hasn't really been that long since he found me in the desert. After his people brought mine to their city, the Fire Clan embraced us with open arms, especially when they found out our species is compatible with theirs.

I stand next to my mate as we watch the Ambassador to the Wind Clan cross the room to greet us. He bows low before straightening.

"My prince," he greets Varus, then turns to me. "Princess, I've just returned from the Wind Clan territory. Your friend, it seems, was indeed taken by a member of the Wind Clan."

I inhale sharply as worry fills my mind. "Did you talk to her? What did she say? Was it her choice?"

Sadness and concern reflect in his eyes as he shakes his head softly. "Forgive me, Princess, but I was not permitted to see her. The royal family refused to grant me an audience."

I grip Varus's arm. "We have to go get her. We have to—"

He takes both of my hands in his as his green eyes pierce

mine. "I promise you, Lilliana, no male Drakarian would ever hurt a female. That is a crime none of my people would ever commit."

"Then why wouldn't they let the ambassador see her?"

"I do not know. But I can promise you that Prince Raidyn would never harm her." He lowers his gaze in a pensive look. "Perhaps it has something to do with the king—Raidyn's father. It is well known that the king is half-mad. The death of Raidyn's mother broke him many cycles ago. Perhaps he is paranoid that we sent an ambassador to his kingdom to inquire about his son."

The ambassador steps forward. "We will send a message to Prince Raidyn assuring him that his mate's people simply wish to speak with her. To confirm that she is safe."

His statement worries me. An unstable king never boded well in old Earth's history, but I trust Varus. And if he says the Wind Clan won't hurt Skye, I believe him. "You think that will work? That Raidyn will let us see her then?"

"If he does not, we will threaten their Clan with war," Varus replies with a slight clench of his jaw. He turns to the ambassador. "Will you deliver our message?"

He bows low. "Yes, my prince. At once."

My eyes follow him out the door, praying that Raidyn listens to reason and allows us to see Skye. I miss my best friend. She's like a sister to me and I just want to talk to her, to know for sure that she's all right. I remember how scared I was initially of Varus in his draka form. At least, I got to know his humanoid form first before realizing he could shift.

But Skye was taken by a draka—that must have been terrifying. To top it off, she didn't have a translator chip, so even when he shifted back into a man, she wouldn't have been able to understand him.

Varus explained that the only reason I could understand

him when he touched me was because I was his fated mate. So, if Skye is not fated to Raidyn, she would not have any idea what he was saying to her without a translator chip.

The sun hangs low in the sky as I step out onto the balcony, thinking of my friend. Hoping and praying I'll see her again soon.

Varus's warm hands on my shoulders draw my attention to him as he pulls me back against his chest. He wraps his arms around my waist and drops his chin to the curve of my neck and shoulder, inhaling deeply.

"Your scent," he whispers. "It is stronger somehow. More intoxicating. It calls to me more and more lately and I wonder why."

A faint smile curves my lips; I think I have the answer. I turn in his embrace and wind my arms around his neck. Stretching onto my toes, I press my lips to his then whisper against them. "It's because we're going to have a baby."

His brow furrows softly. "Baby?"

"A fledgling," I correct.

His mouth curves in a devastatingly handsome smile as his green eyes seem to dance with joy. He crushes his lips to mine in a searing kiss. When he pulls back, his gaze searches mine. "How do you know? Are you certain?"

I grin. "Yes. I went to see Healer Ranas this morning."

Although I'd been assured by the same Healer not long before that natural conception would be improbable between us without medical intervention, I'm not upset in the slightest. In fact, I'm happier than I've ever been.

Varus lifts me into his arms and spins me around. He presses his lips again to mine while walking us toward the bed. It's no wonder we conceived a child so early in our relationship; he is completely insatiable. We make love several times each night and often during the day as well. He says he's addicted to touching me and I can't complain because I feel the same way about him.

Carefully, he tucks me beneath the comforter and crawls in beside me. He pulls me into his arms, rolling us so I'm straddling his hips. He dips his hands beneath the hem of my robe and slides it off my shoulders, baring me to his gaze. Gently, he traces the tips of his fingers down my abdomen and then places his open palm directly over my womb.

"A fledgling," he murmurs, his voice filled with wonder. A smile crests his lips when he lifts his gaze to mine. "I am happy beyond words, my beautiful linaya."

"Me too. Healer Ranas said we will have to check in with him daily to make sure everything is progressing soundly, but there shouldn't be any reason for worry."

I trail the tips of my fingers along the muscles of his abdomen and chest, guiding his hand to my left breast. I move my hips against his and he inhales sharply before he grips my waist firmly and stills.

I frown. "What's wrong?"

His brow wrinkles in confusion. "You wish to mate before you nest?"

"Nest?"

He nods. "Yes, to lay the egg. Drakarian females refuse to mate until after they have laid their egg."

A soft laugh escapes me. "There won't be any egg."

He cocks his head to the side.

"My people carry their young until they're born, remember?"

"Yes, but since the child is mine, I thought that—"

I shake my head to cut him off. "Ranas said I will carry our fledgling to term in my womb. He doesn't suspect that I will go over your species' six moon cycle. However, since our baby is the first Drakarian hybrid, he's not entirely sure."

His expression dims slightly, and he carefully crawls out from under me. He wraps his arms around my waist and tugs me close, pressing a soft kiss to my forehead before gently moving away. "Of course. I vow that I will not pressure you into a mating. We will wait until after our fledgling is born. My vow."

My mouth drifts open and I shake my head again. "Humans aren't like Drakarian females, Varus. We can mate for almost the entire time that we're carrying a baby."

His brows shoot up to his forehead. "You speak truth?"

I nod.

He lunges for me and before I know it, my head hits the pillow. He rolls me onto my back, moving so fast I barely have time to catch my breath as he captures my mouth in a searing kiss.

I shift slightly beneath him to cradle his hips between my thighs. A soft moan escapes me as he runs his hand down my body to cup my left breast. When his stav enters my channel, he groans low in his throat, fixing me with a possessive gaze.

"You are mine," he growls. "My beautiful and perfect mate."

He strokes long and deep inside me. As his shining green eyes stare deep into mine, that's exactly how he makes me feel—like I am everything to him.

I've never been happier.

Varus thrusts deep inside me and I cry out his name as waves of pleasure overwhelm me. His release follows mine and fills me with warmth. He holds me close as we reach our climax together, his body pressed against mine. The steady rhythm of his hearts is a comforting reminder of his strength and his love for me and our child.

When my people set out on the colony ships, I never imagined we'd end up on a planet full of Drakarian warriors.

However, meeting Varus's eyes full of love and devotion, I cannot imagine being anywhere else. I don't know what the future holds, but as my mate gently presses his palm to my lower abdomen and smiles brightly, I know that I'm eager to meet it.

ABOUT ARIA WINTER

Aria Winter

For information about upcoming releases Like me on Facebook (www.facebook.com/ariawinterauthor) or sign up for upcoming release alerts at my website:

Ariawinter.com

Other books from Aria coming soon:
Elemental Dragon Warriors Series
Claimed by the Fire Dragon Prince
Stolen by the Wind Dragon Prince
Rescued by the Water Dragon Prince
Healed by the Earth Dragon Prince
Once Upon A Fairy Tale Romance Series
Taken by the Dragon: A Beauty and the Beast Retelling
Captivated by the Fae: A Cinderella Retelling

Rescued By The Merman: A Little Mermaid Retelling

Once Upon a Shifter Series
Ella and her Shifters

ABOUT JADE WALTZ

Jade Waltz lives in Illinois with her husband, two sons, and her three crazy cats. She loves knitting, playing video games, and watching Esports. Jade's passions include the arts, green tea and mints — all while writing and teaching marching band drill in the fall.

Jade has always been an avid reader of the fantasy, paranormal and sci-fi genres and wanted to create worlds she always wanted to read.

She writes character driven romances within detailed universes, where happily-ever-afters happen for those who dare love the abnormal and the unknown. Their love may not be easy—but it is well worth it in the end.

Website: www.jadewaltz.com
  Facebook Group: Jade Waltz Literary Alcove
  Twitter: @authorjadewaltz
  Instagram: @authorjadewaltz
  Email: authorjadewaltz@gmail.com

Also By Jade Waltz:

Solo Works:

Project Universe Timeline:

Project: Adapt #1 – Found
    Project: Adapt #2 – Achieve
    Project: Adapt #3 – Develop

Project: F5 #1 – Bird of Prey
    Project: F5 #2 – Scaled Heart